LAURENCE YEP

Sea Glass

GOLDEN MOUNTAIN
CHRONICLES: 1970

■ HarperTrophy®
An Imprint of HarperCollinsPublishers

Sea Glass
Copyright © 1979 by Laurence Yep

Library of Congress Cataloging-in-Publication Data
Yep, Laurence.
    Sea glass.
    p.   cm.
    Summary: A Chinese-American boy whose father wants him to be
good in sports finally asserts his right to be himself.
    ISBN 0-06-441003-X (pbk.)
    [1. Chinese Americans—Fiction. 2. Fathers and sons—Fiction.
3. Sports stories.] I. Title.
    PZ7.Y44Se   78-22487
    [Fic]

Typography by Karin Paprocki
First Harper Trophy edition, 2002
❖
Visit us on the World Wide Web!
www.harperchildrens.com

To Spike and Terry,
who put up with a great deal

Thirty years ago, I began writing stories about one family, the Youngs of Three Willows Village, and their many friends. In those pages, I tried to chronicle their ongoing love affair with the Land of the Golden Mountain, or America—a love that has lasted over one hundred fifty years.

The first Youngs came to the Golden Mountain because they had no choice: It was the only way for their families in China to survive (*The Serpent's Children* and *Mountain Light*). However, their children realized that the Golden Mountain was—despite hardship and death—their destiny (*Dragon's Gate*). And so the third generation was actually born upon the Golden Mountain, sinking their roots inextricably into American soil—despite the attempts of hostile American mobs to tear up those roots (*The Traitor*).

The Youngs and their friends stayed even when the many rural Chinatowns that had once covered the West were destroyed and Chinese America itself had shrunk to a few small enclaves in cities like San Francisco. However, that didn't stop a new generation from immersing itself in American thought and technology in order to achieve its dreams (*Dragonwings*).

More than everything else, the Youngs and their friends were adaptable, even organizing their own professional basketball team to leave San Francisco's Chinatown and barnstorm across the country (*The Red Warrior*). However, some went too far and became so American that they lost track of the Chinese part of their identity and had to discover it again (*Child of the Owl*). And they changed once more when they discovered that the attitudes that had enabled them to survive over a hundred years of hardships and dangers no longer worked (*Sea Glass*).

Ultimately, the latest generation—which is only half-Chinese—faces the greatest challenge, for it has to redefine what it is to be a Chinese American (*Thief of Hearts*)

It has been my privilege to write about seven generations of the Young family and their friends, and how they have transformed the Golden Mountain and been transformed in turn. These books represent my version of Chinese America—in its tears and its laughter, its hungers and its fears, and in all its hopes and dreams.

KO, the forty-ninth hexagram of
the *Book of Changes*

"Superior people shed their skins and transform."

CHAPTER | I

I

"Hup-one."

I think when Bradley grows up, he's going to become a tank. Correction: He already is a tank. But maybe when he's eighteen, he'll let the army paint him olive drab and strap a cannon to his nose.

"Hup-two."

It felt funny to be playing football on this big a stretch of lawn. In Chinatown, up in San Francisco, we had played our games mostly on the tennis court of the playground, or if that was occupied we played on the basketball court. The closest thing we had to a field was a stretch of lawn that was maybe twenty by thirty feet in one of the housing projects in Chinatown. Or if we wanted to walk into North Beach, there was always Washington Square—though sometimes there was trouble with some of the Italian kids.

"Hup-three."

Italian kids. White kids. Black kids. Kids like Bradley. But the only other Chinese boy down here in Concepcion was my cousin Stanley, who was a year older than me. All the other boys were Americans and bigger than us, though Bradley was the biggest.

"Hike."

When the center snapped the ball, I went straight for Bradley's stomach with my left shoulder and arm. You'd think that something as big as a sofa pillow would be just as soft, but his stomach felt as hard as the front of a tank. I dug my feet into the dirt and tried to drive forward, but I might just as well have been trying to push a tank back. And then Bradley went from neutral into first gear and I could feel my feet begin to slide back through the grass. And then he shifted into second gear and I almost lost my balance, but I managed to step back in time. I twisted to the side to body block him, remembering to bend my arm over my ribs to protect them while I tried to hit his legs; but by that time Bradley was into high gear and it was like trying to roll against a charging tank. I was just too light and I got knocked onto my back.

Then there was this giant-sized sneaker right over

my face. I could see the Keds imprint still on the sole. And for a moment I thought Bradley's size-twelve sneaker was going to be my last sight of the world. I put my hands up and felt Bradley step on my forearms, pushing them against my face.

I rolled over on my stomach and tried to scramble to my feet, which made me just in time to see Bradley grab Jim, the quarterback. Lucky for Jim we were just playing touch football or Bradley would have casually dismantled him. As it was, Bradley just got Jim in a bear hug and shook him around a little.

I got up slowly from the grass with the knees of my pants now a bright shade of green. I felt like quitting right then. Only I told myself that I couldn't let Dad down.

I mean, I'd made this promise to Dad the day after Christmas when we'd moved down here from the City. The three of us had been sitting in the cab of Uncle Lester's old pickup truck. Dad was driving, I was sitting in the middle, and Mom was by the other door. Every now and then she'd twist her head around and poke it out of the window to check on the things we had tied in the back.

Then, once we reached the mountains before Concepcion, all my favorite rock stations on the radio faded away into static. No matter how much I fiddled with the dial, all I could get was this one station that played such great hits as "Ricochet Romance." Finally I just turned off the radio in disgust. "I can't get anything."

"No rock music?" Dad asked. "Good. Maybe your eardrums will get a chance to heal." Rock music was one of the few American things that Dad didn't approve of.

"I like it." I shrugged.

On a straight stretch of the highway, Dad glanced at me. "We're moving in with *Western people*, you know." *Western people* was a Chinese term Dad and Mom politely used for white Americans. "You can't waste the whole day listening to that noise. You got to get out and prove you're just as good as one of them." He adjusted the steering wheel of the pickup truck. "You got to remember one thing, Craig: A Chinese has to try twice as hard as any *Western person*. You got to study twice as hard. You got to play twice as hard. You got to be twice as friendly. Or you're just some dumb Chinese F.O.B."

"F.O.B.?"

"Fresh off the boat," Dad explained.

"But I was born here. So was Mom. And you've lived most of your life here. So did your father."

"That doesn't mean anything. You stand next to some white kid who came here a year ago from Europe and

4

they'll still call the other kid an American and they'll call you the foreigner. They'll only accept you as an American if you can be twice as good as them. Otherwise, you're the stupid Chink who isn't going anyplace."

"I think," Mom said carefully, "that Craig will do just fine."

"No," Dad insisted. "Craig, you got to play hungry. You got to study like you're hungry."

I looked at Dad. "What do you mean by 'hungry'?"

Dad took one hand from the steering wheel and pretended to snatch something from the air and grasp it tightly. "'Hungry' is wanting something so bad that it hurts inside."

I was going to say that I didn't want anything, but Mom poked me with her elbow. Whenever Dad explained his philosophy of life, I wasn't supposed to question him—no matter how strange it might sound to me. So instead of arguing with Dad, I just stared straight ahead out of the window. "I'm too fat to play hungry," I said.

But even without that pep talk from Dad, I would have known that it was important to make a good impression on the other kids. I trotted back toward the quarterback, who was walking backward and looking around the field. "Whose man was that?"

I held up my hand. "Mine, sorry."

"Sorry doesn't do it." He pointed at another kid. "Ralph, you take Bradley."

By that time my cousin Stanley had come back to the huddle. He was so fast that he always played end. "I was in the clear, Jim." He spread out his hands. "It was six points for sure."

Jim studied the grass for a moment. Without lifting his head, he whispered. "Well, let's do it again." He raised his head suddenly to look straight at me. "Only this time I want some protection."

When we lined up the next time, Ralph lined up before Bradley; but Bradley shifted positions with the other rusher in midcount. Bradley didn't even look at me but just kind of stared through me, like I was a window, and he was looking straight at the quarterback, poor Jim. I kept my head up and drove for Bradley's stomach, but Bradley grabbed handfuls of my shirt. When he started to throw me to the side, I tried to trip him. Bradley clipped me pretty good on the side of my head then. Well, fair was fair, so to speak.

When I got back to the huddle, Jim was kneeling on the grass, rubbing his sides with his hands. "Jesus, I think Bradley broke something. Why don't you guys give me some protection?"

The center shrugged. "I got my man."

"And I got mine," Ralph insisted.

"It's my fault, I guess." I looked around guiltily.

Jim just ignored me, which I think was worse than if he had said something. It was like I wasn't worth an insult. Then he gave a little grin. "Let's do something they won't expect." He nodded to me. "Let's throw to him."

"My name is Craig."

"Yeah, well, you go out, see"—Jim traced a straight line across the grass and then moved his hand toward his left—"and you hook over the middle—"

"I can't catch," I said.

Stanley, my cousin, looked up at the sky like he was praying. Then he looked back to Jim. "He's right. We tried to throw the football around once when I visited him in San Francisco."

Stanley was a year older than me. Until I had moved down to Concepcion, about the only thing I knew about Stanley and his sister, Sheila, was that they were both one big pain. At the family banquets in Chinatown, they were always asking for knives and forks and wanting Coca-Cola to drink instead of tea.

Down here, they lived in the newer part of town. Their father was an engineer and their mother was a registered nurse, so they were pretty well off. Even though we had been in Concepcion for a week and a half, this was the first time I had seen them down here. Stanley smoothed the patch of dirt before him. "Don't throw to Craig." He began to trace a line in the dirt. "I can run a post pattern——"

Jim held up a hand. "Hey, who's quarterback?" He stared at me intently. "I won't throw anything fancy. You just go out"——he nodded to me——"and count to ten and then turn around and I'll lay that football into your hands as soft and gentle as a baby's bottom." He nodded to Stanley. "You stay back and help Ralph block out Bradley."

Stanley didn't look very happy at that.

I lined up before Bradley; but when the ball was snapped, I stepped around him as he charged. I ran out about ten yards and turned around. No one had picked me up.

I don't know. Maybe I really could have played a lot better if I hadn't been so worried about disappointing everybody; but I was usually thinking so much about not being a failure that only half my mind was on the game itself.

Then Jim threw the ball up high and soft and I waited.

Even though Dad wasn't there watching me, I felt like he was. I could remember how angry he had sounded during our football practices. I told myself to loosen up. I tried to keep my arms bent. Elbows in against my sides. Look the ball into my hands and then guide it into my body. And all my muscles started tightening up until my arms and legs and fingers felt as stiff as poles and wouldn't do anything that my mind was desperately telling them to do.

When the ball finally seemed to float in front of my face, I tried to squeeze it as a drowning man would grasp at a life preserver. And to my dismay, I felt the ball's rough hide just go squirting between my hands. It bounced off my chest and went dribbling along the ground.

I trotted back to the huddle. "You blew it, man," Stanley said angrily. "It was as clear as a country road upfield. A sure touchdown and you blew it, man."

Nobody said anything else to me in the huddle. We had to punt now, and this time Ralph came over to help me with Bradley. And on defense, I told them that I wanted to rush. It was the only thing I could do. I was just too slow and clumsy to do anything else. Up in Chinatown, where I'd been one of the heaviest kids, it'd been all right. But, of course, down here they had

Bradley blocking me. It wasn't like running into a brick wall—it was a lot worse. I mean, brick walls don't move and brick walls don't climb all over you. The rest of the game went that way.

All in all, it wasn't the best way to get to know the other kids on my first day in school. Bradley, though, was decent enough, considering that he had personally used me to rake up most of the field. When the buzzer sounded for the end of noon recess, he came over to give me a hand getting up. "You've got hustle, you know that?"

"Yeah, but that's about it." I rubbed at the corner of my right jaw where I'd caught somebody's foot.

"Well, if football isn't your game, maybe baseball or basketball is."

I didn't know how to tell him that football was—or rather had been—my best game. I hunted around in my mind for something else to say to Bradley, when he turned his head away from me to listen to what someone else was shouting. Before I could say anything more to him, he'd wandered off. Well, he was in Stanley's class. I suppose a ninth grader wouldn't have much use for an eighth grader.

I drifted over toward Stanley. Stanley spun the football as he threw it up in the air and then caught it.

"Good game," I said to him.

Stanley grunted something.

"Ever come to Chinatown much—I mean, Concepcion's Chinatown?"

Stanley did his best to ignore me. In my nervousness I went on talking. "We got this house, you know? Or, I guess it isn't a house. It's really just a flat above the store. But it's the first time we've ever had a building to ourselves." In fact, Mom and Dad were pretty proud of it.

"We don't go into that part of town much," Stanley said.

"It's Chinatown, man."

"So?" Stanley shrugged.

"Well, you ought to go down there. I mean . . ." I didn't know how to express my feelings to Stanley, and with a superior smile on his face he watched me struggle with the words.

It was almost a relief to have Harold interrupt me. "Hey, Stan, your ass was grass today."

"No blocking, man." Stanley didn't look at me, but Harold did. He laughed and said something to Stanley. Stanley wouldn't even look in my direction—like I was some big embarrassment to him.

For the next few minutes, I laughed along with them whenever either of them told a joke, but they always

11

interrupted me before I could finish saying anything. I just started feeling stupid standing there—pretending I was part of their group. I mean, I really wasn't. I hadn't done anything like Dad had wanted me to do. And the worst part of my day was still ahead of me when I had to go home to face Dad.

II

When we had come to Concepcion, I hadn't been expecting any San Francisco, but I did expect more than a strange little town. When we had first driven down from San Francisco in the truck, we had come into the newer, eastern part of Concepcion. There, all the houses looked like they had been thrown together overnight. They all looked the same, and their walls and shingled roofs looked more like plastic than concrete or wood. The lawns were all neatly trimmed and the hedges clipped. And every house seemed to come equipped with one father and one mother and one boy and one girl. I felt like I'd been shrunk down and gotten stuck in one of those little toy towns that they set up around the electric trains in the department store windows at Christmastime.

The older part of Concepcion may have had more character, but it also looked more tired. The houses in this part of town were of stucco and had curved Spanish tiles on their roofs, so the houses looked like old Spanish villas that had shrunk with old age. There were junk piles by a lot of the houses too—old chairs, old tin cans, even old sofas outside the houses on the squares of dirt that served as front yards for the houses. If there were cars in the driveways by the sides of the houses, the cars were usually without wheels, their axles resting on wooden crates and left dangling like animals with amputated legs. And the ground, from the street across the sidewalk and up the alley, would be covered by big patches of black oil. The whole place looked like some mysterious sea of junk had washed through the streets just that night and beached these things around the houses and then withdrawn.

The one bar on the street had screens over the windows and the doors, though that day there wasn't any glass left except for bits scattered on the sidewalk. They crunched under my feet. An American in a cowboy hat stood in the glassless window sipping from a can of beer. He raised it in a salute to me as I passed by.

There was a poker place next to the bar. They didn't have any glass in the windows either, so I could see the cheap scarred tables where people could play for "fun" though everybody knew they played for money. Next to the poker place was the flophouse where most of the farm workers stayed when they had the cash.

When I passed the flophouse, I was in Concepcion's Chinatown. It wasn't much if you were used to the one up in San Francisco. I mean, there weren't more than four buildings to Concepcion's Chinatown. One of them was a little cafe with an owner who was practicing to be a mass food poisoner. Another building was a two-story pink concrete place with a balcony on the second floor enclosed by a bright green railing. It belonged to the Chinese Chamber of Commerce, but it didn't get used much. Across the street was a small hotel, with a big sign saying "Peace and Prosperity Hotel," where the dozen or so old Chinese men stayed. Uncle Lester's Victory Grocery Store was the last building in Chinatown.

My dad had told me that Concepcion's Chinatown used to be a lot bigger. That was when there were a lot of farms that the Chinese used to run, and any Chinese who wanted to get a job working on them had to come to Concepcion. Dad said there used to be Chinatowns all over California, but then the old guys had quit or died or gone back to China. The ones who were left were the ones who did not have enough money to return.

There were a few old-timers who remembered Dad when he had lived in Concepcion as a kid—before my grandfather had started a business up in San Francisco and they had moved up there. But there wasn't really any kind of social life in Chinatown for Dad and Mom. The Chinatown here was dying. I mean, Mom, Dad, and I were the youngest people in Concepcion's Chinatown.

Living in Chinatown in San Francisco had really been like living in a small town. You knew each other from the time you were kids, and there were Chinese basketball leagues and tennis tournaments and dances—just about every kind of thing that the Americans enjoyed the Chinese did too, but inside or near Chinatown. Chinatown had been home, but Dad and Mom had turned their backs on all that. Now all they really had were themselves and me. Dad and Mom could have tried joining some organizations or churches down here, but Dad said he was too tired to go out at night and Mom wouldn't join anything without Dad.

I knew something was up when I saw the bright, spanking-new, gold Mustang parked outside the store. The car had those fancy mag wheels and thick, cushiony seats and a little compass-thermometer on the dashboard so you'd not only know what direction you were going in, you'd also know how cold it was. I could see two speakers above the backseat, so I suppose it had a stereo set too.

"Craig," Mom called. She was standing in the doorway

with her arms folded. She was a short woman with a pleasant oval face. She kept her hair cut short and carefully curled. "Guess who's here."

"Must be somebody rich," I said.

"It's Uncle Tim and Auntie Faye," Mom said brightly. Uncle Tim was Mom's brother and Stanley and Sheila's father.

"But I thought Sheila and Stanley were still back in the school yard." I hoped they weren't here right now. I had this sinking feeling like the sidewalk had suddenly dissolved underneath my feet and I was just about to fall. I mean, I didn't care all that much for Stanley and Sheila, but I had tried to make friends with them. Only they'd been real snobbish. To my relief, Mom shook her head. "No, it's only your uncle and aunt. Why don't you go up? I've already had my turn."

Our store wasn't very big. It was maybe about thirty by forty feet, with a red concrete floor. There was a long, narrow storeroom that covered one side and a small back room with a sink on the side next to the storeroom. I went through the back room and stepped into our backyard. At least Dad called it a backyard, though it was only a twenty-by-twenty-five-foot rectangle of concrete. Then I took the back stairs that led up to our flat. Mom had hung out some washing to dry on the clothesline that hung over the garden.

The flat wasn't very big either. It had only one bedroom, where Mom and Dad slept. I had a sofa bed in the living room. Besides a couple of tiny closets, a bathroom that was only a bit larger than the closets, and a kitchen, there wasn't anything except the front stairs that led down to the street. But it was the first time we had ever had so much privacy. Up in the City, we'd had this apartment on the second floor, so we used to get noise from above, the sides, and below.

Standing in the kitchen, I could hear Dad's deep voice booming from the living room, so I headed for there. Uncle Tim was a round, satisfied-looking man, while Auntie Faye was a small, very fat woman with a pinched, tight-lipped face that always looked very pained if she had to smile. She liked the gloomy side of things, you see. As some of our relatives said, there wasn't a silver lining that she couldn't find a cloud for.

I left my books on the kitchen table and stepped into the living room. "Dad?" I asked.

Dad twisted around in his chair and waved me into the living room. "Say hello to your uncle Tim and auntie Faye."

"Hi," I said to them. I stood uneasily beside Dad.

Dad leaned back in his chair. "It's a shame that you

couldn't bring Stanley and Sheila along to play with Craig."

"Sheila had to go to that practice with a precision swimming team," Auntie Faye explained.

"And Stanley"—Uncle Tim beamed—"well, he's on just about every team. Up till last year he was in Little League baseball, though this year he's too old so he'll have to join the Senior League. And he's on a Pop Warner football team. He's on a playground basketball team. You name the sport and he plays it. He's got trophies, medals"—Uncle Tim shook his head—"and MVP awards like you wouldn't believe. And you know what?"

"What?" Dad asked.

"Guess." Uncle Tim nodded his head toward Dad.

"I can't," Dad said impatiently.

"Stanley gets straight A's too." Uncle sat back happily. "A real all-American boy. Popular too. Friends are always calling him to visit them."

"Craig's the same way." Dad held my arm affectionately for a moment.

I would have liked to die right then. It was bad enough messing up during the football game at noon. But now I could just imagine Uncle Tim and Auntie Faye going home and having Stanley tell them just how lousy I was.

Uncle Tim folded his arms across his chest. "Craig, you look just like your old man, you know that?"

"Thank you," I said.

"That's nothing to thank him for," Dad said, but he seemed pleased.

Uncle Tim studied the mantelpiece. Suddenly he jumped up. "Hey, that's the old high school basketball team." He went over to the mantelpiece and picked up the old photo in the wooden frame. He smiled to himself while he looked at it. "Your dad used to be a big man in our high school, did you know that, Craig? Especially after he made All-City," Uncle Tim glanced at me. "The first Chinese kid who ever did that. The newspapers called him the Champ of Chinatown."

"Dad is a good player," I said. Mom had shown me the old, faded newspaper articles that she had clipped from the newspapers.

"The guys on the team all did pretty good too, you know?" Dad said. "Augie's a banker. Chuck's a lawyer. Everybody did okay."

Uncle Tim tapped a solemn, chubby face in the photo. He gave a low chuckle. "That's me. The team manager. I got all the dirty towels."

"I would have just left those things when we moved." Dad gave an embarrassed laugh. "It was Jeanie's idea to bring all that stuff down here. I had to make her take along her medals as well. She tried to tell me it would just make more stuff for her to dust, but I said I'd do the dusting there."

Mom's track medals were there, mounted on a velvet-covered piece of cardboard and protected by a frame.

"Yeah, I remember." Uncle Tim leaned against the mantelpiece and stared at Mom's medals. "Whenever we were at the Chinese Olympics, Jeanie used to win everything." For a while, they used to hold a track-and-field meet named the Chinese Olympics. They may have had other events, too, but it was the track events that I had heard about.

"But," Auntie Faye said, "those are all old trophies."

"We don't want to overdo it," Dad said.

Auntie Faye raised an eyebrow. "But you ought to have something up there that Craig's won."

"I haven't won anything," I said quickly, before she could ask any more questions.

Uncle Tim turned. He waved the photo at me. "You must have won something. Don't be shy. Your dad and mom used to win everything in sight."

"Sure, sure." Dad squeezed my shoulder lightly. "He's just a chip off the old block."

That made me feel even worse. I mean, I could just

imagine what Stanley would say to Uncle Tim and Auntie Faye when they got back home. Stanley would tell them about how much I'd screwed up in the football game and then Uncle Tim would say that it was too bad that I didn't take after Dad and Mom. Then all of them would feel sorry for my parents. And if Uncle Tim got together with any of Dad's old friends, he'd tell them about me so they could all feel sorry too.

I thought I ought to try to set the record straight right now. Maybe then we could end this line of conversation. "I'm not too good at sports. I'm too fat."

"That's what comes of all that city living," Uncle Tim said. He pinched my arm. "Wait until you get out to play with Stanley. We'll work some of that fat off."

"Craig's just kidding you. He's a fine player," Dad insisted, as much for me as for Uncle Tim. "He just has to learn not to play so tight."

I turned to look at Dad. He was smiling uncomfortably at Uncle Tim. I would have liked to have asked right then if Dad really believed that or if he was just saying those things to fool Uncle Tim; but, of course, I couldn't ask Dad with Uncle Tim around. However, considering what Dad said in our practice sessions, I decided that Dad must have been telling a small white lie. After all, Dad was the Champ of Chinatown. How could he have a son so lousy at sports? He had to say something to the people he had grown up with.

Dad snapped his fingers. "You know, maybe Stanley would come over and I could give him some basketball lessons along with Craig."

Uncle Tim glanced at Auntie Faye and then he replaced the photo on the mantelpiece and returned to the sofa. "That would be nice," Auntie Faye said diplomatically.

"Well, how about it then?" Dad asked eagerly. "I mean, maybe it would do Craig some good to have Stanley helping him too," Dad said. I wanted to crawl right underneath the rug at that moment. "Let's say tomorrow after school."

Dad really seemed to want to include Stanley in our practices. I guess if he had Stanley there, he would enjoy himself more. When Dad practiced just with me, I only seemed to make him madder and madder.

"Well—" Uncle Tim began uncertainly when Auntie Faye touched his arm.

The corners of Auntie Faye's mouth twitched upward for a moment and it seemed to hurt her to do that—like someone had just sunk a pin into her arm. "It's just that Stanley is so busy. We don't want him to get tired."

"Oh, sure, sure." Dad wagged his leg impatiently. He sounded real disappointed. Instead of coaching just me, the lousy player, Dad must have been hoping to have Stanley as well. I guess he wanted to coach some good athlete. Some real all-American kid.

CHAPTER | II

I

Later that afternoon, long after Uncle Tim and Auntie Faye had left, I was in the back getting a six-pack of beer to put into the store refrigerator when I heard the POING, POING, POING of a basketball on the concrete floor. I hated the sound. It meant a basketball practice. We had begun with football practice at first; but after a few days Dad had given up and switched to basketball.

I know that most kids would have jumped at the chance to goof off and shoot some baskets with their dads, but for them it was just fun. For me, though, it meant something else. It wasn't just that I disliked having to do something I wasn't good at. There are plenty of times in school when you have to practice something that you're not good at and never will be. What really got to me was what these practices meant for Dad and what he wanted them to mean for me. To Dad, a practice was more than teaching me how to put a round sphere through a metal ring. Mom had tried to explain it to me when we had first moved down here.

You see, Dad had had all these plans for us. Before he would let us go upstairs to look at the place where we would be living, he had insisted that we follow him into this tiny, narrow, concrete courtyard next to the store. The courtyard was formed on one side by the store and on the opposite side by the house next door that belonged to a Mr. Lopez. Fronting the street was a high wooden fence with barbed wire strung over the top to keep people from climbing over. The fourth side consisted of a toolshed and a narrow opening that led into the alley where the garbage cans were.

"Here it is." Dad waved his hand with a big flourish.

"Here is what?" Mom asked. We looked around at the lifeless little rectangle. I thought it was one of the gloomiest places I'd ever seen. If you wanted to see if the sun was shining, you had to lean way back and crane your neck up to see the little patch of sky caught between our store and Mr. Lopez's house. That day, even though it was a clear, sunny day outside, there in the courtyard the sky looked like an old blue sheet somebody had hung out to dry.

"This is going to be our backyard. See, there's a fuchsia plant growing there." Dad pointed to a long, narrow strip of dirt about a yard wide that ran along-side Mr. Lopez's house. A big bushlike thing grew there, but there were no leaves or blossoms on it and its bare branches looked spindly.

We walked over to stare at it. "Is it dead?" I asked.

"No-o-o." Dad smiled and drawled out the syllable, letting his voice drop lower. "It's through blossoming now." Delicately he felt one slender branch between his thumb and forefinger.

Aside from the fuchsia plant, the only life in that little courtyard was us—and any bugs that might have been hiding in all the junk back there. Uncle Lester seemed to have used the place mainly to store away things like the big old cans that used to hold a hundred pounds of rice, or empty wooden soda crates. I was standing in just a gloomy, junky, lifeless little rectangle of dirty concrete. The walls of the store, shed, and fence were painted a dull gray like you see in the movies on the walls of a prison, but at least in the prisons the paint looks new; the paint on the wall of the store had fine lines in its surface, like the wrinkles of an old man's face, where it hadn't peeled away already. And even though Mr. Lopez's house had been painted white, it must have been a long time ago because the paint was flaking even worse than the paint on our store.

All in all, it seemed to me like it was a nothing place we could have just as easily skipped; but it was like Dad was standing in some other place altogether. He pointed at the strip of dirt. "Your mom could have fruit trees there," he said to me. "When they're grown, she can pluck an apple whenever she likes." Dad pantomimed plucking something from a tree.

I looked at Mom. It was the first time I'd ever heard that she liked any kind of tree.

Mom sighed and shrugged. Then she looked around at the shadows filling the "backyard." "Is there enough sunshine?" she asked doubtfully.

"Sure, sure." Dad hardly seemed to be listening to Mom while he made his plans. His lips were pressed together as if he were thinking, and there was an absent, peaceful look to his face like I'd never seen before. It was as if he were dreaming happily. "Or maybe we ought to have flowers instead. Yeah, in flower boxes." Dad crossed quickly to a stack of empty wooden soda-pop crates. He picked one up and inspected it critically. "Sure." He lifted his head to look at Mom. "I can take out the dividers for you and we can use this crate for a flower box. In fact"—Dad set the first crate down on its side as he leaned forward to check the next crate—"you could use them all." He counted the crates. "There's three here. You can have a garden."

"Shouldn't we concentrate on the store first?" Mom suggested tactfully.

Dad turned. For the first time he seemed to notice Mom's frown. Dad could be stubborn about a lot of things, but not with Mom. He held his hands away from his sides. "It won't take too much work," he coaxed, "and then it'll be nice back here when you take a break."

Mom couldn't help smiling. "And give you an excuse to get away from the store and come out here to work."

"I won't need an excuse. I'll like the store." Dad nervously fingered the zipper on his jacket. "It's for you, you know. I just thought that you'd like a garden."

It was always Dad's way that whenever he wanted to do something, he always said it was for one of us— when neither of us had ever expressed a wish for it. I mean, for instance, we'd always been satisfied with the one radio in our apartment up in San Francisco, but Dad had got it into his head to take a correspondence course in radio and TV repair. For a while we had been ankle deep in broken radios that Dad had found or been given. He had always insisted that he was going to fix every one of those radios. (He never did get even one of them to work.) Of course, all of the radios were going to be repaired for us. It was like Dad was afraid of being put down if he had said one of the radios was for him.

I don't think Dad's excuses ever fooled anybody except himself; but his intentions were usually so good that we wound up giving in to him.

It happened again in the backyard. Mom forced herself to smile as if she were pleased. "It would be nice to have a garden."

"You're sure now?" Dad asked.

"I'm sure," Mom said. She had to act as if she really wanted it now.

"I didn't know you liked gardening, Dad," I said to him.

"Don't you have cars, boy?" Dad slammed the first crate back on top of the stack. "I said it was for your mom."

From behind his back, Mom shook her head for me not to say anything more.

Dad turned around and stopped when the toolshed caught his eye. He pursed his lips thoughtfully again. "You know what?" He crossed the concrete quickly to the shed. He stretched his arm up and just touched the roof of the shed. "I'll put up a basketball hoop right here on the side. It won't be regulation height but we could practice." He winked at me. "We'll make you into the next champ for sure."

"Unh, thanks, Dad," I said, not very enthusiastically, "but I always got along okay before now."

Mom frowned at me like I had said the wrong thing.

"Sure, you're okay—considering that we never had many chances to practice together." Dad held up his fore-finger and thumb, holding them apart just slightly for emphasis. "But with just a little work, we could make you an All-City player." Dad smiled at me encouragingly. "Maybe even an All-American."

I began to protest that I didn't want to be any of these things, but Mom grabbed Dad's arm. "I'd like to have the others up in Chinatown see what we have down here. They're all cooped up in those little apartments."

"Yeah." Dad's smile broadened. "I feel sorry for them. People should have flowers and trees. Not cable cars and bus fumes."

I didn't know the first thing about flowers or trees, but I did know about cable cars and buses. In fact, I liked them. They had always been part of the fun up in the City, because they would take me anywhere that I wanted to go. And now Dad was putting them down. "You always used to like cable cars before this," I said.

"Why don't you like them now?"

"We never had any choice before this." Dad ignored my hurt look.

But Mom noticed, and the first chance we got to be alone, we sat on the floor of the living room and we talked. "What's the matter?" Mom asked. "You don't like it down here?"

"Not much. It's not like San Francisco at all."

"I know," Mom said, "but we have to give Concepcion a chance."

I shrugged. "Yeah, I know that. I guess what really bothers me is the way Dad's acting. I never said I wanted to be an All-American; and you've never said that you wanted a garden. But he's going to give us that stuff whether we like it or not."

Mom leaned her head against the wall. "You didn't grow up when we did. Some *Western people* used to say to us, 'You're Chinese. You're foreigners. You don't belong here.' It used to hurt inside when they said those things to me." Mom wriggled her fingers as if she wanted to get the circulation going in one of her hands. "But your dad showed them. Nobody thought a Chinese could make All-City varsity, but he did." Mom glanced down at me. "Your dad could play any *Westerners'* game and beat everyone."

It made me feel a little proud inside. I could feel a kind of pinching at the corners of my eyes like I wanted to cry. "So they didn't call you a foreigner then?"

"Well, not as many did, anyway."

Finally, I said, "But that was then. What's that got to do with basketball practice? Or fruit trees? Or a garden?"

Mom shrugged. "I guess it's what your dad thinks every American family does or has; and naturally he wants those things for us too."

"I always thought he was doing a good job before we moved down here," I said. "I was always satisfied."

"I know. So was I," Mom said. "But your dad thinks he can do more for us. We should go along with his dreams. Do you understand what I'm saying?"

"I guess." I scratched the side of my head nervously. "It's just that a couple of times when Dad had the day off and he took me down to the Chinese Playground to shoot baskets, it wasn't much fun. I just seemed to make him angry no matter how hard I tried."

"The practices mean a lot to your dad," Mom insisted. "Basketball was how your dad made his American friends. He wants the same thing for you."

"But maybe I could make friends in other ways. Why do I have to do it his way?"

"You have to remember that your dad never had that much to do with his father except when he was helping him in the store." Mom smiled patiently. "So maybe he's trying to help you the way he wanted his father to help him."

"Sometimes," I said carefully, "I wish he wouldn't try so hard, you know?"

"Yes, I know that feeling very well." Mom gave a toss to her head and laughed a little. Then she spread her hands apart. "But you just remember something else. It's real easy to make him think he's doing a bad job as your dad. He acts like he's so sure about things, but he really isn't. Inside, I think he feels like he's a little boy pretending to be someone older and bigger. A cheap person might make your dad feel bad. But you're not cheap, are you?" Mom nudged me encouragingly.

I sighed. "I guess I can give it a try."

"Good," Mom said. "That's all I can ask."

But let me tell you: It wasn't easy being the all-American boy that Dad wanted as his son.

Dad finally appeared in the doorway to the storeroom. "Hey, the Champ of Chinatown's here."

"Can we shoot baskets later? I ought to put the beer into the refrigerator."

Mom came up behind Dad. "I'll do that. You go ahead."

"Come on, Craig. If you don't practice, you'll get rusty." Dad's voice had a coaxing tone to it. I thought of how he'd had to listen to Uncle Tim brag about Stanley, the real all-American boy. Maybe Dad had thought he had to make me into someone he could be proud of. And I remembered again how I'd promised Mom that I'd make Dad feel good.

I set the six-pack down. "Sure. Let's shoot some baskets."

I led the way into the "backyard."

Dad had tried so hard to make that ugly, lifeless courtyard into a garden. He'd dumped the old tires and junk into the shed and knocked the wooden partitions out of three soda crates with his hammer and filled the crates with dirt from a vacant lot to make the crates into flower boxes. Then, next to the store, he'd placed an eight-foot-long plank on top of some old empty rice cans and put the flower boxes on top of the plank.

I'd watched Dad as he'd poked holes into the soil with a screwdriver and planted a flower seed in each hole. Opposite the flower boxes, in the strip of dirt alongside Mr. Lopez's house, he'd scattered grass seed so we'd have flowers on our right and a lawn on our left.

Every day after that, Dad had disappeared into the backyard for an hour to tend the garden. Then, three days ago, Dad had locked the front door to the store and dragged Mom and me into the backyard to show us there was a green shoot in each of the flower boxes and about six green blades of grass just peeping out of the dirt underneath the fuchsia plant.

I hadn't seen what all the fuss was about. Both the grass and flower shoots were so tiny that we'd practically had to put our noses into the dirt before we could see the tiny dots of green against the black soil. But Dad couldn't have been prouder if we had owned Golden Gate Park. I'd tried my best to copy Mom and admire the "garden," though it was kind of like trying to admire the dozen hairs on top of a bald man's head. I mean there just wasn't that much for me to get excited about, especially when no new shoots appeared after that. I was afraid Mom was right: The courtyard was too shady to grow much of anything.

Today, as he stepped into the backyard after me, Dad let the ball drop; and when it rolled over the top of his foot, he kicked it up in the air and behind him, where he caught it with one hand. Then he began to dribble again—all without breaking step. Dad had been a Chinese All-Star a long time ago. Back before the world war, for a few years, they had organized a Chinese basket-ball team to play games, like the Harlem Globetrotters. And Dad, who had been tall for a Chinese, had played forward. In Dad's hands the basketball came alive as if it were his pet.

I walked over to the flower boxes. "Anything new?" I asked. I could put off the basketball practices for a little while if I could get Dad to talking about his plants.

"Maybe." Dad dribbled the ball along slowly until he had joined me and then he let the ball bounce away. "What's happened?" He bent over close to the flower boxes. The little green shoots were all withered, and the dirt stunk. "Cats," he said, almost spitting out the words. "They've gone on our plants." He whirled around. "They got the lawn too."

I glanced back at the sad little flower shoots, almost feeling sorry for them. "Maybe they'll get better."

Dad shook his head disgustedly while he got the basketball. "They're dead. Or close to it."

I wished I could have gone upstairs right then. Between the talk with Uncle Tim and Auntie Faye and the cats killing the plants, Dad was going to be in a lousier mood than usual.

Dad crouched and began to dribble, waiting for me to try to guard him. He never tried any of his fancy stuff on me when we played one on one. "Get your hands out, boy," he snapped. My mistakes always seemed to make him so angry.

"Right, Dad." I tried to sound as conscientious as I could, but it didn't take the angry frown from Dad's face. He always got that way in our practices—like he always expected so much and I always gave him so little.

I threw my arms out and squatted a little. He didn't have any trouble pivoting. His right arm went up over his head as he hooked the ball into the air. The ball clunked through the rim and bounced with a deep hollow POING from the concrete back into Dad's hands. You would have thought that it would have made Dad relax more, but he still frowned. "Remember. Get your hands up too." He sounded even more annoyed—like I'd let him down again.

"Right, Dad." I put my arms up in the air for a moment to show that I would remember. Then I had to put my hands down quickly when he tried to pass the basketball to me. The basketball went right between my hands and bounced against my chest. Even so, I managed to clutch it with my arms.

Dad grunted and went down into a guard stance. I would have preferred just to take a shot from there, but I knew he wanted to see if I could drive in.

"Remember what I told you." He gestured impatiently toward my legs. It would have been hard to forget, since I'd spent one hour each day for a week learning the moves.

"Right, Dad." I pivoted, pretending to pass to my right. Dad obligingly shifted over to try to cut off the pass. Then I pivoted and pretended to pass to my left. Dad went over to cut off that pass. "Come on now," he said in an irritated voice. "Drive. Faster, boy! Faster!"

"Right, Dad," I said. I tried to drive in, but my dribbling just wasn't up to it—no matter how much I practiced. The ball bounced too high and I couldn't quite control it. Actually, I wound up more chasing after the basketball than dribbling it. But Dad stayed to the side, watching. The basketball finally got away from me and hit the side of the toolshed, meaning it had gone out of bounds. It rolled in against the fuchsia plant and I picked it up. In a way, I was thankful. Yesterday when I had tried a lay-up, I had missed the rim entirely and put the ball on the roof of the shed, so we'd had to get a ladder before we could retrieve the ball.

Dad looked kind of disgusted with the way I'd tried to drive in to the basket. "Did you make any friends today?" Dad asked in the same rough voice that he would use for asking me if I had picked up my clothes from the floor of the living room.

"I met . . ." I panted, trying to get my breath, "some of the kids." I passed the ball to him.

"Then bring them by." Dribbling the basketball, Dad started to edge slowly to my left and I went with him. "In the City, you had friends coming by all the time."

I didn't know how to tell Dad that Concepcion was different from San Francisco—especially after Uncle Tim had bragged about how popular Stanley was. "Maybe I don't feel like company," I said. I kept a careful eye on Dad, and when he started to edge to his right, I followed him.

"Your hands, boy. Your hands," Dad growled. Embarrassed, I stuck my hands out again. Dad stopped and glanced at me over his shoulder to see where my hands were. Then he whirled around on one foot while raised his other leg and started one of his hook shots. This time I raised my hands up quickly, and Dad the ball against my right hand, which is probably what he meant to do—that way I could have the satisfaction of blocking at least one of his shots. But he threw the ball so hard that it made my hand numb. "Good boy," he grunted and smiled. The ball rolled against his foot. He kicked the ball lightly, and it popped into the air and fell into my outstretched hands.

"The *Western people* giving you a hard time?" Dad demanded. Dad meant it as a sympathetic question, but somehow his face and voice weren't meant for showing sympathy. His voice was meant for shouting orders over the noise of a crowd during a basketball game, and his face had only two real expressions: a slightly annoyed scowl and a truly angry scowl. So somehow when he asked me that question, he sounded more like a coach interrogating one of his players about breaking training and eating a candy bar. I mean, Dad made it sound like it was my fault.

"It's not that." I started to dribble. "It's just that we don't have much to talk about." POING. POING. POING.

"What do you want, boy? A debate team?" Dad snorted. "You gotta get to the playground. Basketbal Football. Baseball. It doesn't matter. Nothing like good game to make the other kids respect you. An once you get their respect, you can make friends re; easy." He sounded a little worried. "You gotta do wh; I did."

I couldn't look at Dad. I guess the Champ of Chinatown wanted to pass his crown on to his son.

"Yeah, I know." I went on dribbling.

"What you said to your uncle Tim about being fat—"

"It's true." I lifted my head quickly.

"Well, we can work that fat off you." Dad shook his finger at me. "But I don't want you using your fat as an excuse to quit. My boy would never quit." Dad sounded as if he were accusing me of some crime like murder.

"Right, Dad." I started to dribble in toward him, and he went into his guard stance. But I was getting kind of tired of playing as if I were going to be the next Champ of Chinatown. So instead of trying to drive in like Dad wanted, I shot from where I was. The ball bounced off the side of the shed above the rim. I just stood there and watched.

"Come in for the rebound. Hustle! Hustle!" Frustrated, Dad waved his hand at me.

"Right, Dad." Anxiously, I started forward. He let me run past him and get the ball as it bounced high off the concrete. He came over to guard me only after I had taken a second shot. I missed again, though I was real close to the basket. Dad let me rebound the ball and take a third shot, and this time I made it. It was just as well, I suppose, since we would have been at it the whole afternoon until I evened the score with Dad.

"That's it, boy. That's it." Dad pounded his hands together so the little backyard rang with his applause. I rebounded the ball, feeling embarrassed.

Dad slapped me on the shoulder. "Man, oh, man. The kids are going to call you a real sharpshooter."

I knew Dad meant to encourage me, but he didn't have to act so excited about one crummy little basket. But Dad was carrying on so much that I was more ashamed of the basket I had made than of all the ones I'd missed. I couldn't win whatever I did.

I gave a big sigh. I had had my fill of embarrassments that day. "Maybe Mom needs a hand," I said hopefully. "Let's stop practicing now." I passed the basketball to Dad.

Dad seemed a little disappointed that I didn't want to go on practicing anymore. "Don't worry about it." Dad rested the ball on top of his index finger and gave the ball a spin. It whirled there on top of his finger. I bet he could walk all around the block while the ball went on twirling. "Do you like it here, boy?"

Managing a store sounded like a better deal than it was. This wasn't any giant supermarket. It was a dinky little store that had to count every penny. Dad got paid a straight monthly salary for managing the store, but it wasn't much for the twelve to fourteen hours he and Mom had to put in every day. And he knew he had to show a profit. Uncle Lester, friend or not, had too many expensive tastes to keep a manager who was running the store into the red. Dad had actually made more as a janitor. But we did get meat wholesale. And there were some snacks. If you felt like some salami at midnight, you just went down the back stairs into the store and cut off a slice, or a small chunk—though too much snacking, as Dad reminded us, would cut into the profits. Anyway, Mom and Dad liked it though it meant long hours.

Maybe if I had had a day to talk to Dad I could have made him understand just how much I missed Chinatown, but it was hard to decide on what I missed the most. It was a lot of little things—like being able to walk from Chinatown to a half dozen movie theaters with first-run American or Chinese shows. And the places for food. And the comics. And the kids.

"I miss my friends a little," I said cautiously.

"That's to be expected."

Actually I missed my friends more than just a little. Even beyond the fact that we knew and did the same things together, like the pay telephone where you could make free calls or the late evening games in the basketball court—I didn't mind playing basketball with them—or taking the bus out to the park and playing war. Or like the time when the Boy Scout troop—I wasn't a scout, just a guest—had gotten lost in the botanical gardens.

What I really missed was a feeling of being whole. I just didn't feel like the same person I had been in San Francisco. As soon as the old truck had finally left San Francisco, I had felt as if someone had ripped off one of my arms.

"But do you like it here, boy?" Dad repeated his question.

"I don't think we'd ever get our own flat up in the City," I said.

"No, we couldn't. And we couldn't have our own garden." Dad nodded his head to the crates.

"Sure." But I'd never wanted a garden or a flat. I wanted a Chinatown, where I fit in so well.

"And you and me, we couldn't get to shoot baskets as much as we do."

"Yeah, I know." And I'd never wanted to shoot baskets. But Mom said we had to go along with what Dad thought we wanted, so I didn't say anything.

Dad threw the ball to me. "You really need more practice dribbling."

"Yeah, I guess so. But Mom's probably beginning to get busy. Don't you think we both better go inside?"

"All right." Dad shrugged. I knew I was disappointing Dad, and it made me feel even worse than before, because he was trying to help me in his own way. I should have at least tried to dribble the ball down the alley, but that would have been too much humiliation in one day so I just carried it. Somehow all of our father-to-son talks always made me feel worse, because I always seemed to let Dad down in some way.

I wondered if Dad would have shouted at Stanley the way he did at me.

II

So maybe I wouldn't do so good during the game. At least I told myself I wouldn't give up. I mean Dad had said no son of his would quit. But the football game the next day went pretty much like the first one had. It was almost a relief when the first buzzer sounded that we ought to begin to head for class. It wasn't so much that I liked schoolwork, but it was the one thing that I did all right. My English might not have been very good, but I could be pretty good at arithmetic and even at history with all those dates and stuff. At least that hadn't changed when I'd left Chinatown. In the classroom, I could be sure of myself and have things become clear for a while: like watching all the sediment settle out of a broth until it's almost as clear as crystal.

Most of the other classes had gone inside, but our teacher, Mr. Loeb, was late for some reason, so most of the kids in my class just kind of stood around outside.

Waiting there and looking around, I suddenly had this strange empty feeling inside me. Everything in Dana Junior High was so spread out. There was so much playing area and the classrooms were all just one story. Like someone had taken a proper three-story school in the City and squashed it flat to make this funny-looking place.

Then Sheila, my other cousin, pushed past me with her two friends, Betsy and Tisha. Sheila was thirteen, so she was in the same class as me. Like her brother, Stanley, Sheila was small but quick and agile and coordinated, so that her hands and feet always did what she wanted them to do. She had her sweater tied around her waist. "Quit hogging all the room, will you?" She sounded especially annoyed with me.

"There's plenty of room," I said.

"Not with you around." The other girls giggled. Encouraged, Sheila went on. "You play funny. You run funny. You even stand funny."

"What's so funny about the way I stand?" I demanded.

"You stand like a pregnant duck," another girl said. Her name was Kenyon. Though Kenyon went out of her way to wear plain, ordinary skirts and blouses like the other girls, she had this frizzy red-gold hair that kind of looked like a small bush. It was as if from the neck down, Kenyon tried her hardest to be like the other girls, but from the neck up she was a different person. She was always saying something funny, so there were usually kids around her.

Kenyon paused and then added, "In fact, we ought to call you"—she drawled out the syllables as if she were announcing them—"Preg-gy Crai-gie." She pointed down at my shoes then. "And those are Preggy Craigie's Wedgies."

The other girls laughed at that. Betsy nodded to me. "Hey, I saw you delivering groceries last week. How come you use that crummy little wagon? It's so rusty you can hear the wheels creaking all over town."

Tisha spoke up then. "How can people stand to have food delivered in that? Why don't you use a bicycle or something?"

Sheila smiled in a superior way. "Preggy never learned to ride a bike."

There had always been buses and cable cars to ride up in the City. I could ride for a nickel each time when I used my bus ticket. I knew almost all the bus routes, so I could get from Ocean Beach on the west to the bay on the east, and from Fisherman's Wharf in the north down to Candlestick Park in the south. But in this dumpy town you were as likely to see a polar bear as a bus—though it wasn't much use trying to explain that to the yokels.

Betsy straightened up from the water fountain, wiping her mouth with the back of her hand. "There are three-wheelers. Jensen's delivery boy uses one of those."

"We don't own the store," I tried to explain. "We only run the store for Uncle Lester, and we have to keep the expenses down."

"Preggy'd still manage to fall off, wouldn't you?" Sheila took her turn at the water fountain.

I could understand the *Western kids* making fun of me; but I couldn't understand why Sheila would join in so heartily. Even if she hadn't been my cousin, she was a Chinese like me. But it was Sheila who insisted on using that nickname the most. It was as if she had to go out of her way to prove to the others that she was different from me.

Still, I thought I'd try to be friendly. "I haven't seen you in Chinatown," I said casually.

"Why should you?" Sheila turned the handle under the fountain and began to slurp at the water bubbling from it.

I stood there, feeling awkward as I tried to explain myself. "Well, you know, I thought you might come down and buy some Chinese stuff for dinner sometime." Up in San Francisco, the Chinese would come into Chinatown even if they lived far away from it. It was the center of their lives.

But Sheila looked at me as if she were staring at the biggest fool in the world. "I'm an American," she insisted.

"Every one of us is an American, but even so . . ." I let my words trail off and hooked a thumb through one of the belt loops on my pants. I gave a little shrug with one shoulder. I mean, we did have more or less the same color in our skin, hair, and eyes. I thought that meant we would have gone through similar experiences and maybe looked at the world in the same way. Even though I couldn't have told you much more about what it meant to be Chinese, I felt like Sheila and I ought to have something in common.

I said in my own slow, clumsy Chinese, *"But everybody ought to go there. You can at least buy toppings to put on rice."* The cafe sold some stuff. It wasn't very good but it was all there was.

"What?" Sheila sounded annoyed.

"Don't you understand the language of the T'ang people?" I

should have asked the question in American, but it made me feel smug to see the blank look on Sheila's face.

"Ah so," Betsy said to Tisha.

"One Long Hop," Tisha replied in a singsong voice.

Sheila clenched one fist. "Talk American."

"You know, people come to Chinatown to buy *toppings.* The stuff you eat with rice. Cashew chicken. That kind of stuff." I put one hand on my hip. "What's the matter? Don't you know Chinese at all?"

"Why should I?" Sheila twisted the arms of her sweater, which was still tied around her waist. "I'm an American, even if you aren't." Her friends had gone on making singsong noises, and Sheila looked like she wished I was dead right then and there. "Why don't you go back to where you belong, Preggy?"

"I belong here now," I said angrily. I was mad enough to use Chinese. *"And how can you say things like that to me, hunh? Even if I weren't your cousin, you and me, we're people of the T'ang."*

"Speak American, will you?" Sheila asked. "You're over here now, Preggy."

"I was born here. Just like you," I said quietly.

"Then why don't you get some decent clothes." Sheila started to turn to say something to Kenyon.

I pulled at Sheila's arm. "What's wrong with my clothes?"

"Gee-zus K. Rist. What's right with them?" Kenyon asked. "No one wears black and yellow and red shirts."

"It's part of the design." I pointed at my shirt. The black outlined the red and yellow squares in big, broad lines. My mother had made the shirt when she had still been sewing in one of the sewing-machine shops up in San Francisco. "I like it," I said.

"It's tacky." Kenyon sniffed. "And it's too big." She cocked her head to one side as if I were some kind of bug she was studying. "And you know what? With your head shaved like that, you look like a little fat Buddha."

Sheila was the first to laugh at that. She was also the loudest.

I found myself rubbing the top of my head nervously. "My head isn't shaved," I tried to say. "It's a flattop haircut."

"Ohhh." Kenyon drawled out the word. "When are the planes going to land?"

"You can't be an aircraft carrier," Sheila said. "They don't take Buddhas in the American navy." She looked around at the other girls and seemed pleased when she saw them all laughing. We were making so much noise that Mr. Prichett, the principal, came out of his office.

"Uh-oh. Let's get inside," Kenyon said. Kenyon raised one hand and waved at me with just the fingers. "Bye-bye, Buddha Man." She went inside, followed by Sheila and the other girls.

So Kenyon had given me another name. If there had been a rock handy, I think I could have crawled underneath it. I was typed as a foreigner just as Mom and Dad had been when they had been in high school; but I didn't have Dad's athletic ability to make the others accept me.

It was going to be a long winter.

III

But if the kids thought of me as a foreigner, the old Chinese here thought of me as an American. I was working in our store after school putting up soup cans. First, though, I had to mark the tops of the cans with a grease pencil—the kind that wrote with a special black filler to mark metal as well as paper. Uncle Lester kept his soup cans in bins in the back of the store. The cans were laid on their sides in neat rows. The store was so old that I wasn't sure what the bins had originally been used for.

Anyway, I was marking the cans when an old, hunched Chinese motioned impatiently to me. He was bent over so far that the trunk of his body almost paralleled the ground. I sighed and got up to see what he wanted.

All the old Chinese were fussy about what they ate, wanting things as fresh as possible, but sometimes they tumbled the fruits and vegetables around so much during their search that they did more damage than could ever be made up by what they bought. This man was one of the worst, always arguing about spoilage and going through the leaves of a lettuce to show us why in all decency we should sell it to him cheaper. I knew the old-timers had to make their money stretch, but sometimes it seemed like they argued just to give us a hard time.

He rattled off something quick and in one of the other dialects, so I couldn't pick up what he was saying. I could understand a little Chinese if it was spoken slowly. He jabbered something at me again. In my own slow, painstaking Chinese, I asked him to speak slower because I couldn't understand him when he talked so fast. He waved his hand disgustedly at me and started shouting something out loud, turning in different directions as if he were trying to get someone else.

Mom was upstairs cooking dinner, but Dad was in the storeroom. He came out now, nodding his head and smiling in greeting to the old Chinese. Dad said something and then ducked back into the storeroom and returned a moment later with a jar of Tiger Balm, which is a kind of salve. He had asked Uncle Lester to bring it down from San Francisco on his last visit. There wasn't any profit in it. Dad did it as a favor to the old-timer, though he didn't seem to appreciate it much.

The old Chinese opened up an old, worn coin purse and grudgingly counted each coin into Dad's outstretched palm. During that slow process the old Chinese kept talking all the while. The smile froze on Dad's face and his spine kept getting straighter. I could tell Dad was getting madder and madder. Every now and then the old Chinese pointed at me. I kept laying the soup cans in the bin.

Finally, when the old Chinese saw he wasn't going to get any reaction from Dad, he turned to me. "You shou' be ashame." He nodded his head firmly. "Ashame. You shou' learn Chinese." He spoke English very slowly, as if his tongue and mouth were wrestling with each syllable. "You young Chinese. You shou' know Chinese. You shou' act Chinese."

He went on like that for a while. I just put on a stone face for the old man, a blank expression that showed I didn't care. Methodically I started to mark the bottom layer of cans. Finally, the old Chinese shook his head, muttering as he shuffled toward the door.

I felt kind of numb inside as I put the new cans into the bin. Funny, I'd always used the word "Americans" for whites, and "Chinese" for myself; but I guessed Chinese really didn't apply to me. I was more like a white American than anything else, even if my skin was the wrong color. It was a shock. It was as if I wasn't anything anymore. Neither white nor brown, but some funny, hollow, tan-colored balloon that had been made in the shape of a human and had been towed around by my parents wherever they went.

When the old man was finally gone, Dad came back to where I was. "Don't pay Ah Joe any mind. He's just crazy. They used to say the same thing to me."

"Yeah?"

"Sure." Dad grinned. "All the time."

"What happened to his back?" I put the last can into the bin. Then I started to open the flaps of a new case.

"He used to be a laundryman, and between bending over to work and his arthritis, his back got that way." Dad added, "You know, some of the old-timers used to call me lazy and say I was wasting my time by playing *Westerners'* games. They used to talk about how it was different in China." Dad put his hand into his pants pocket and jingled the change there. "Only the China most of those old-timers remembered even at that time wasn't there anymore. If it ever was."

It was nice of Dad to say those things, but it just seemed as if I couldn't make it as a Chinese. After hearing old Ah Joe scold me like that, even the Chinatown in San Francisco would seem different. I'd always be wondering what the old-time Chinese would be thinking of me.

I felt like I didn't fit in anyplace anymore.

CHAPTER | III

After that incident with Ah Joe, I wasn't very comfortable with any of the other old-timers. But the one old-timer who really got to me was this spooky one I never got to see for week after week. His name was Uncle *Quail*. Of all the grocery deliveries I had to make, going to his cottage was the longest and the hardest trip, so I always delivered his groceries last in the afternoon.

Dad had delivered Uncle's groceries alone the first time and stayed a whole afternoon to visit with Uncle. (Dad had lived in Concepcion until he was twelve. Then, when my grandfather had started a business up in the City, Dad had moved there.) The next time, though, Dad had just shown me the way without actually going down with me. After that, Dad had left the deliveries up to me.

I thought of Uncle *Quail* as some kind of ogre after

Uncle Lester's stories. Uncle Lester, who actually owned the Victory Grocery Store, was only a friend of Dad's and no blood relation to us; but he had said that his uncle *Quail* was a blood relative—something like a great-uncle or even a great-great-uncle. Uncle *Quail* had always been here as far as Uncle Lester knew, and Uncle *Quail* had always been one of the store's liabilities—like the mortgage, the leaking roof, and the mice. You see, Uncle *Quail* received his groceries for free.

Every week I brought him the same things from the list. There were cans of peas and soup, and a small bag of rice, and other things like sardines and seven cigars. Uncle always wanted yams—fresh when they were in season, otherwise he took canned ones. There also had to be a freshly killed chicken. Uncle Lester had instructed Dad to pay a nearby farmer special to bring in a freshly killed chicken every week. Dad had to pluck and clean it, though.

I asked Uncle Lester why he didn't give Uncle *Quail* one of the regular chickens like we had in the meat counter; but Uncle Lester warned us that he'd tried it once. The next week when he brought the new carton of groceries, there had been a note written in Chinese inside the carton from the previous week. The note had been so blistering that Uncle Lester was too embarrassed to repeat it to us.

Anyway, during all those months I had been delivering Uncle's groceries, I was kind of grateful that he hadn't come out to talk to me.

Then came that one Saturday in April.

It started out like any other trip. First, I had to go through the part of the town that was one of the oldest; the street was shaded by big poplar trees whose roots tilted up the sidewalk sections so that the slabs looked like the waves of a stormy sea that had been frozen suddenly. It wasn't any fun pulling the wagon up and down the slabs of sidewalk. But the fun really began when the sidewalk came to an end, and I had to pull the wagon along the dirt road.

On either side were rows of neat, whitewashed little cottages with shingled roofs, all exactly alike, which were used only when the summer people were in town. At the end of one row was the tidiest cottage, surrounded by a white picket fence to protect the rosebushes.

"How's by you?" old Mrs. Koch called. She wore a big floppy straw hat to shade herself from the sun and a man-size pair of gardening gloves that used to belong to her husband.

"Fine, Mrs. Koch. How's everything with you?" I kept on going because you're dead if you ever let Mrs. Koch stop you. She'll keep on talking for hours.

She considered that for a moment while she picked some of the dirt from her trowel's point. "All right, I guess. Taking him his groceries?"

"Yessum," I called over my shoulder.

"Funny man." Her voice grew louder as the distance between us increased. "He was here already a long time before my Henry built our cottages. And that wasn't exactly yesterday."

"Yessum. Well, 'bye now," I shouted, because I was almost out of earshot.

It was a strange thing, but in our neighborhood there weren't too many who had been born in California. And only Mrs. Gonzalez had lived in Concepcion all of her life. A lot of our neighbors had moved here from other states to find work, but even more were old people like Mrs. Koch who had come here to retire. Mr. Koch had been a colonel in the army when he finally left it. He'd come to live in Concepcion and had built the summer cottages that he rented out. Mrs. Koch ran things now that he was dead. The only time that Concepcion ever jumped with any life was during the summer, when people came down from San Francisco.

Past Mrs. Koch's, I crossed the Coast Road and hauled the wagon across the big gravel-filled parking lot. It went for several acres down toward the south. The parking lot was completely empty. The sand drifted in over the concrete breakwater to form a little dune on the parking lot. Nobody bothered to sweep it away during the winter and spring. Sometimes on a sunny day, sitting on the benches by the breakwater, the old people would talk, their creaky voices lost under the big sky. But on a day as cold as this, there wasn't anybody out there.

When I reached the cliffs on the north side of the parking lot, I stopped and took a breath before I started up the sandy path that zigzagged to the top. A dirt track led across the top of the cliffs, and I pulled the wagon along past the brown weeds and the scraggly windblown trees that grew there. I stopped by the old rusty wire-mesh fence. The gate was unlocked, as it always was on Saturdays. The open padlock hung to the side on one of the wires.

Carefully I lowered the wagon down the stone path to Uncle's house. Uncle lived on a small cove about fifty feet across that was formed by the cliffs and a headland. The rock had crumbled at the mouth of the cove a long time ago, maybe in some storm when the heavy waves had come crashing in, and now lay piled across it to form a reef that protected the cove from the rest of the sea—except for that one narrow opening in the reef. Right now it must have been high tide, because only the top of the reef showed.

There was only a little strip of beach at high tide, and I couldn't see the wooden pilings where Uncle used to have a small wharf. A stone path wound up the cliff wall behind the beach for about fifty feet before the path widened out to a ledge about thirty by forty feet. It was there that Uncle had built his little wooden cottage. The paint had worn off long ago, leaving the wooden planks exposed to the wind and the salt spray so that the wood was a grayish color and smooth as the surface of a skull.

There were shades over the windows, shades so old that they looked an orange-goldish color. Sometimes I thought I saw one of the shades stir—like an eyelid twitching. And I would have this spooky feeling like someone was watching me.

I would always shove the new carton of groceries and bunch of the past week's Chinese newspapers onto the porch. Then I'd take the old box, which was filled with garbage that Uncle had wrapped neatly in last week's newspapers. I'd put the box into the wagon and I'd tear back up the path with the almost-empty wagon rattling and bumping along behind me.

But today it was different.

I had just put the carton of groceries on the porch of Uncle's house when the door suddenly opened and an elderly Chinese in his seventies stood there.

On his feet he had a pair of Chinese slippers with dragons embroidered on the front. His legs were encased in a pair of old gray work pants that sagged like elephant legs. Over a torn T-shirt, Uncle wore an old green jacket that came only to his waist. The lining on the inside obviously had once been of bright bands of yellow, red, and green in some silklike material, but the coat was torn now at the bottom, and though Uncle *Quail* had tried to mend it, the material had been too old and worn, so that his jacket had torn again, letting the padding begin to trail out once more.

He held out his hand to me and said something in Chinese, but too quickly for me to understand. Then he spoke more slowly, barely able to contain his impatience. *"Quick, boy. I want the* sardines." The last word was in American.

When I just stared at him, he gave a little contemptuous sigh and dug around in the carton himself, scattering cans left and right onto the porch. I looked over the railing down at the cove fifty feet below his house. A small shadow circled underneath the surface of the water.

"What's that?" I asked in Chinese. I turned back to Uncle. He had pried the key off the bottom of the can and fitted it onto the metal tab on the top. Then he began

to wind the entire lid down.

In the meantime, the creature had surfaced so I could see it was an otter. Funny, but the otter looked like old Mrs. Koch—if her face had been covered with brown fur. He stared at us for a moment; then he began to clown in the water, rolling and spiraling and tumbling.

"*Quit showing off,*" Uncle pretended to scold the otter. With a flick of his wrist, Uncle threw a fish up high into the air. It glittered as it fell through the sunny afternoon air: a silvery flake that splashed into the water near the otter's head. The otter dove, surfacing to float on his back with the fish between his humanlike paws. He ate with big nods of his head as he gulped it down.

Uncle wiped his fingertips on the seat of his pants and glanced at me. "*You want to try it?*" He held the can in front of me. I slipped a sardine out and threw it. It almost hit the otter on the stomach. He looked so surprised and indignant that Uncle and I both had to laugh. It didn't seem to bother the otter, though, because he dove for the fish. We took turns feeding him after that. The otter seemed to realize when the tin was empty, because he began to circle the cove.

I watched him slide around in the water. It was hard to think of him as flesh and bone. He curled around so fast and darted away that he seemed more like a brown streak that someone was trying to paint on the water, only the water kept on shrugging off the paint. It almost hurt inside me to look at him. That otter was so sleek and fast and graceful—everything I had ever wanted to be and wasn't. I held on to the porch railing so I could lean far out to catch one last glimpse as he shot through the narrow opening in the reef at the mouth of the cove and out into the open sea. And then I couldn't see him anymore.

Uncle said something more in Chinese.

"Pardon me?" I asked.

Uncle spoke in American. "I said he's very beautiful." He switched back to Chinese. *"What's the matter: Don't you speak the language of the T'ang people?"*

"Only a little," I confessed. I waited for him to begin ranting like Ah Joe had done.

Uncle grunted like he wasn't surprised in the least at my stupidity. "You speak. You act. You even think like a *white demon.*" By *demon,* he meant an American. With a very stern expression on his face, he stared at me.

I was more intimidated by Uncle than I had been by Ah Joe. Though Uncle *Quail* was in his seventies, he still moved quickly and yet gracefully—as if his body could barely contain all of his energy. His hair, which he cut short on top and almost shaved on the sides and back of his head, only accented the bullet shape of his skull. His shoulders were still broad and heavily muscled.

"Well, *little demon*, someone squeezes my bread too much." He made wringing motions with his hands as if he were twisting the water out of a wet towel. "Is it you?"

"I guess I just grab it too hard when I'm in a hurry." I rubbed nervously at a patch of dirt I'd gotten somehow on my left elbow.

"I only make toast with it anyway," Uncle said, "but I don't want toast that is all twisted. How you like it if I pay you with bent coins, hunh?"

"I'll be more careful the next time," I promised.

"I wait and see." Uncle clasped his hands behind his back. "What's your name, boy?"

"Craig. Craig Chin."

"Ah." Uncle scratched for a moment behind his ear. "Are you Calvin's son?"

"Yes, sir."

"He and Lester, they used to bring my groceries. Just like you, hah?" He waved his hand back and forth between me and him. "But that was a long, long time ago." Uncle paused as if he were searching for something else to say. "Your father was strong. Even when he was small. Very strong." Uncle closed his hands into fists and pretended to make his muscles bulge. "He always play the *demon* games even then."

Even down here I couldn't escape from Dad's reputation. "Oh" was all I said.

"And you? You like the *demon* games?" Uncle asked kindly.

"Sort of," I said without much enthusiasm. Somehow, whenever I got to talking to people about my dad, they always wound up asking me if I liked sports. They assumed not only that I did, but that I would be as good at them as Dad had been. I went on quickly. "But I'm not very good at sports." I glanced at the box with Uncle's garbage neatly wrapped in newspaper and began to think of excuses for leaving.

But instead of going on with his questions as other people would have done, Uncle was silent. When I turned around to say good-bye to him, I found him studying me. There was a fine network of wrinkles around his eyes, but I hadn't noticed them before because his face had been more or less relaxed. Now, though, his forehead was wrinkled and his eyebrows were drawn together, and there was a deep, intense look to his eyes. For a moment, I felt more alive: as if I ought to be like the sunlight leaping from the back of one ocean wave to another.

Then Uncle blinked his eyes and the look slipped away from his face. He smiled at me reassuringly. I felt the corners of my mouth turn up into a brief, uneasy grin. It was as if Uncle understood that I didn't want to be asked any more questions about how good I was at sports.

For a long time, neither of us knew what to say to the other. Finally Uncle faced toward the cove. "You . . . you like my friend?"

I could only nod my head in agreement. We had something to share after all. I think that fact pleased the both of us. "Does the otter come here often?"

"That lazy thing? He only comes when he feels like it. One of these days, no more fine meals from me." Uncle did his best to sound as if he disapproved of the otter because he begged for food. It was actually, as I was to learn, just Uncle's way never to compliment anything wholeheartedly. Uncle added sternly, "It's a waste of good food."

Even so, I knew he ordered two cans of sardines every week, because I was the one who filled his order for groceries. It was written on a scrap of butcher paper in pencil that had gotten smudged over the months. I suppose Uncle had dictated the list to his relative, Uncle Lester.

"Will the otter be back today?" I asked Uncle.

Uncle scratched the side of his nose. "I not think so." He added, as if he didn't know what to do with me, "But you can wait if you want."

"I guess I could stay a little while." I sat down on the porch and began to pick up the cans that Uncle had scattered all around while he had been hunting for one of the sardine cans. As neatly as I could, I put the cans back into the carton.

Uncle picked up the seven cigars from the porch where he had tossed them earlier. Then he sat down carefully on the porch beside me. He stretched one leg out stiffly and rubbed it as if it ached. With his other hand, he stowed six of the cigars in a jacket pocket. Finally he unwrapped the seventh cigar and bit off one end, spitting out the little mouthful. Then he reversed the cigar and stuck it into his mouth. Clenching it between his teeth, he hunted around in his pants pocket and took out a book of matches. His other hand groped around on the porch until it found a black ugly shell by the left railing. The shell was about seven inches long. But when he turned it over, I saw the inside was all silvery, with a beautiful swirl of metallic colors rippling and flowing around the insides as if this were half of a shell that had hatched a rainbow.

While he lit his cigar, I studied the shell in fascination. "Where did you get that?"

"This?" Uncle held up the shell as if he took it for granted. "It's only an abalone shell. No good. Got too many cracks."

"I've eaten abalone. I thought they were fish."

"No, boy." Uncle laughed. He waved his cigar toward the cliff. "In the old days there was a whole bunch of us catching abalone south by Monterey. We cut the meat and put it on trays so the meat dries. Then we send the meat to China. We sell the shells too. Some months you could shut your eyes and just smell the air." Uncle closed his eyes and pretended to sniff at the air. "And you find our camp."

With great care, Uncle slowly took the cigar from his mouth so that the ash stayed there until he could tap his cigar against the side of the abalone shell—it was as if he were playing a game with himself. "Hey, you know what, boy?" He glanced at me sideways. "I find abalone on my reef still." He jabbed his cigar at the air in the direction of the reef. "Someday I take you out there and we dive for abalone." He added, "But you think you could keep it a secret? I don't want everyone down here." He turned and looked at me shrewdly.

"I can keep a secret," I said doubtfully, "but do we really have to swim out there?"

Uncle grunted. "Maybe I see how well you swim. The abalone, they don't come crawling into your hand, you know." Uncle was doing his best to sound disinterested, but I could hear the eagerness in his voice.

Even so, I hesitated. "I don't know." I didn't want to disappoint Uncle, and yet I didn't know how to tell him that I found it embarrassing to go swimming. Once, when we were still in San Francisco, I'd gone to Ocean Beach with some friends, and I felt real stupid there. I'm fat. I wore an extra-big T-shirt to cover up my stomach. And when I sat down, I know the fat on my chest made it look like I had a girl's tits. And my swimming trunks were large ones and they hung down almost to my knees. I felt like all the average, thin people were looking at me and snickering.

Uncle sucked at his cigar and then blew out a large circle. "Don't you worry, boy," he said gently. "Most of the time nobody comes up here, so nobody can see us." It was as if he could read my mind. Sometimes you meet people who like having other people around so they can have an excuse to hear their own voices talking. But as I came to know Uncle, I found that he could understand people—almost as if he could read people's minds and didn't much like what he read there so he usually didn't make the effort. Uncle knocked some more ash into the shell. "You know, it's a funny thing, but I don't like people watching me. A few times people come up to the cliffs, but then I can smell them so I go inside."

I looked down at the seawater surging up the sand.

It was like a thing alive, with gold scales winking and disappearing and reappearing again on the surface. And outside the cove I could see the separate shades of water in the sea. It certainly looked inviting.

But then I let myself imagine what Mom and Dad would say, especially Dad, when I gave them an abalone shell as a decoration for our house. Maybe if I had two, I could show one of the shells to the other kids. I could just picture the kids' faces.

"You do swim, don't you, boy?" Uncle asked.

"I learned in the pool at the Chinatown Y up in the City."

Uncle snorted in disgust. "That's tame water. Nothing to see but chlorine and the legs of other people kicking." He nodded toward his cove. "You take a place like this. Now that's water."

I held on to the railing. "It might be fun to swim here. If it's okay."

"Oh-kay." Uncle made it sound like two separate words. "Next Saturday, when you bring my food." He gave an almost shy little smile.

CHAPTER | IV

That Saturday Uncle was already down on the beach. He looked thin and bony and sinewy as he sat with his jacket draped around his shoulders. I turned the wagon around and pushed it before me through the gate. Then I leaned back on my heels and gently lowered it down the path, trying not to look to my right where the edge of the path was. Uncle didn't look up even though the old wagon rattled noisily down the rocky path.

I lifted the carton of groceries out of the wagon onto the porch, sliding it over toward the door. Then I put the old carton with the garbage into the wagon and parked it against the porch so it wouldn't roll down. One lonely sea gull wheeled about, crying over the calm waters of the cove. "Afternoon," I called down to him. My voice echoed on the rocks but Uncle didn't turn around. He just waved his hand vaguely in the air.

I picked up my towel, which was rolled into a cylinder, and with that tucked under my arm I went down to the beach. The tide was really low today. The beach was a lot bigger and I could see a lot of the reef. At the foot of the path, I began to slog across the sand toward where Uncle sat. "I didn't squeeze the bread this time."

"I wait and see." Uncle had a small crowbar in his hand. It was tied to his wrist by a thong. I watched as Uncle slipped the end of the crowbar between the shell and the tan flesh of an abalone.

"You went diving for abalone without me." I stared at him accusingly.

When Uncle had the crowbar positioned just the way he wanted, he shoved it in hard. I suppose he must have broken the abalone's hold on its shell, because he pried it out easily, dropping it into a basket. "I walk through my gardens and I find this one."

I looked around the cove, but it looked especially empty and lifeless now. Even the gull was off to some other place. There were barnacles on the cliffsides, but they were above the water so they were shut up tight and I didn't think they counted. To me, anyway, it looked like the only living things there were me and Uncle.

"What gardens?" I asked skeptically.

Uncle smiled as if it were his secret. "I thought you were one smart boy. Can't you see them?" He slipped the thong of the crowbar from his wrist and dropped it into the basket.

"No, I can't." Sullenly I folded my arms across my chest.

"You think maybe you see, but you don't. Not really." He pointed at my eyes. "Your eyes, they tell your mind a lot of stuff. But your mind, he's one busy fellow. He say, 'I don't have time to listen. Fill out these forms.' So the eyes, they fill out the forms, but there's no place on the forms for everything they see. Just a lot of boxes they are supposed to mark or not. So your mind, he misses a lot." Uncle nodded his head firmly. "You gotta look at the world. Really look."

"Like you?" I was beginning to feel impatient with Uncle.

"No. I only do it in a small, small way. But if you can make your mind listen to your eyes, really listen, what wonders you see." Uncle looked out at his cove wistfully. "You know *the Dragon Mother*?"

"No," I said reluctantly.

"Now there was some person who saw the world. *The Dragon Mother* was a human once, but her mind listen to her eyes. She go for a walk, like you and me, we do sometimes. But this woman, she see a dragon's egg." Uncle pretended to look down sharply at the wet sand and hunch his shoulders and hold out his hands from his sides as if he had just seen something.

I looked at the same spot on the beach. "Dragon's egg?"

"You know that the dragons are kings of the sea." Uncle tapped my arm with the back of his hand.

I drew away slightly. "Sure, I know something about that stuff. They live in the sea and in the rivers and they bring rain."

Uncle motioned to the spot on the beach where he had pretended to find the object. "Well, this woman, she find this rock." Uncle pantomimed picking something up from the sand. "She go home and show it to her friends. Everyone tell her, 'You're stupid. This is only a rock.' But she say, 'Mind your own business. This is one special thing.' So she dig a little pool by her home." Uncle scooped some sand from the beach with his hand and set down the imaginary object in his hand. "And she put in seawater over the thing. And she change the water every day for a year. And everyone laugh at her. But she keep doing it because she knows it's special even if they don't. And then one day, one day . . . the thing hatches." Uncle stretched his fingers wide above the hole he had just dug.

"But the baby, it's no sea turtle, no other animal. It's a dragon." Slowly Uncle lifted his arms and spread them as if the dragon were growing in front of us. "She raise this little dragon like it maybe her own son. And this dragon, he turn out to be a very important dragon and so humans and dragons, they name her *the Dragon Mother.* She became one important person. And only because this woman, she can see." Uncle dropped his hands back down over his knees with loud slapping noises.

"Oh," I said.

"This is one special place here. This is the edge of the world. This is where the magic can happen too." Uncle searched my face, looking for some sign of comprehension, but I could only look at him in confusion. Uncle smiled to himself sadly. He pretended to become stern. "Well, you want to swim, or talk, boy?"

"Let's swim." I started to undress self-consciously on the beach. I was already wearing my swimming trunks underneath my pants, so it didn't take me long. In the meantime, Uncle had shrugged off his jacket and waded into the water to begin swimming. I stared at him in surprise.

He moved almost as quickly and easily through the water as the otter we had seen. There was nothing wasted about his motions when he swam. It was pure, simple, graceful.

"Come on." Uncle turned to me from the water. "You just remember one thing. The currents in my cove, they aren't very strong, but even so, don't fight them."

I adjusted the waistband of my trunks over my stomach, knowing that the waistband would slide back under my belly before long.

Uncle hadn't shivered or said anything when he'd walked into the water. You'd have thought it was warm bathwater to him. But I gave a yelp the moment I waded into the water. The water felt so cold that it felt like someone had been chilling it in the refrigerator. I could feel the goose bumps popping out all over my skin, and I began to shake and to huddle up and hold myself.

Uncle waved one hand from where he was floating. "Come on. You get used to it."

I nodded nervously and kept on walking. I felt the beach slope downward sharply, and I immediately found myself in the water up to my chest. The sea wasn't very pleasant to move around in, but it was better than that first moment of shock. Then a wave broke against the reef and spray went flying and the sea surged through the narrow opening. The pull of the sudden current wasn't all that strong, but it caught me by surprise so I got knocked off my feet.

I couldn't see. There was only the clouded, stinging salt water all around me. I flailed with my arms, trying to get my feet on something solid, but I couldn't find anything. And then I felt the current begin to draw me away from the beach as it began to flow out toward the sea. I really panicked then, forgetting everything I'd ever been taught. I wanted air. My lungs tried to drag it in, but all they got was salt water. I began to choke.

Then strong hands appeared magically, gripping me on either side. I tried to grab hold of Uncle. Something. Anything, as long as I could hold on to it. Somehow, though, Uncle managed to avoid me. My head broke above the surface. I could see the light for a moment before the salt water, running down my face, made my eyes close. I gasped, coughed, and gasped again, trying to get the film of seawater out of my lungs.

Uncle's strong hands pulled me steadily in toward the beach. Then I could feel firm sand under me. I stumbled. Uncle's hands held me up until I got my balance. I started to stagger toward the beach with Uncle supporting me. Gratefully I felt the air around my shoulders and then my chest and then my stomach. I stretched my arms out like a blind man and stumbled out of the surf to fall onto the beach. I lay on my stomach for a moment, coughing and spitting. I could still feel the sea pulling at my ankles, so I crawled another yard farther up the beach. The sea swept higher. I could feel it tugging at my ankles again, as if it were alive and trying to drag me back in.

Then I felt Uncle's shadow as he sat down heavily beside me. "You sure you can swim, boy?"

I sat up, beginning to shiver. Uncle covered my shoulders with my towel. With one corner of the towel I wiped at my face. "I could have told you. I'm just too fat and clumsy. Sorry."

Uncle put on his ragged jacket and sat down. "You feel too sorry for yourself. And that's not good."

"Are you crazy?" I started to shiver, so I pulled the towel tighter around my neck.

"You're the crazy one." Uncle flung sand over his legs. "You want to stay on the beach when you can be out in the water."

"Drowning isn't my idea of fun." I wiped some of the water from my face.

Uncle put his hands behind him and leaned back. "Well, maybe if you're scared . . ."

With a corner of my towel I finished drying my face. "Who said I was scared?"

"Me," Uncle said. "I say you're scared."

"Nothing scares me," I insisted.

Tunelessly Uncle hummed to himself and tapped his fingers against the sand.

"Well, even if I am," I mumbled, "it's stupid to do something just to prove I'm not scared."

"Yes, no, maybe so. Something good shouldn't scare you." Uncle began to rub his palms together so that the sand sprinkled down. "Maybe I ask you to put your head on a railroad track, and you say no, well, that's different."

"I'm still not going in." I shook my head for emphasis.

Uncle worried at the nail of one finger. Some sand got on his lips. "You can walk on the water then?" Uncle smiled, amused.

I liked Uncle when he said that. I mean, Dad would have gone on shouting or wheedling or both, but instead Uncle turned the whole thing into a joke. He seemed to relax then. "You want to go for a walk instead?" He nodded at the beach. "I mean on solid ground?"

"Sure," I said, even though the cove wasn't more than twenty yards wide at any point.

Uncle rose and started across the wet sand toward the cliffs on one side of the cove, and I followed him. When he was by the cliffs, Uncle pointed to the walls above the water at the foot-wide bands of chalky little white bumps. "These are mussels, and those"—he gestured at a blackish band about a foot wide below them—"are barnacles." The bands looked like they were painted on both sides of the cove where the tide would reach it about a yard above its present level. "The water's out or they'd all be open to eat the little things in the water.

"And you see the starfish?" Uncle pointed at the water where there was a bright orange spot just below the surface. "He's waiting now. When the water get higher, he climb back up to the barnacles and mussels." We waded cautiously into the surf; and, as the water sucked at my ankles, he took my wrist and guided it under the water. I felt the rough surface of the starfish. Uncle let go of my wrist and I traced the shape of the starfish and felt the five legs, one of them curled up slightly. My fingers closed round the body of the starfish and I gave a tug; but it felt as if it were part of the cliff wall.

Uncle laughed in delight, like a kid sharing a new toy with someone else. "You want a starfish, you need a crowbar. Once a starfish sits, nobody can pull it up."

I let go of the starfish. "Is this your garden then?" I looked around the cove, feeling disappointed. The bands of mussels and barnacles and the starfish didn't make up a sea garden in my mind.

"I bet you think this is one real crazy old man, right?" Uncle asked. He bent over so that his hands were near the waterline and ran his hands lightly over the face of the barnacles that were clustered so tightly together. He did it lightly, or the rough faces of the barnacles might have cut up his hands. Suddenly he gave a yelp. He lifted out his hand, and I saw clinging to it a long, greenish-brown worm with lots of legs. And then it let go and dropped with a plunk back into the sea.

"Did it hurt?" I asked.

"No, see, not even the skin's broken." He showed me the finger. "That's the hunter that stalks and kills, and this whole place is his jungle." He indicated the bands of mussels and barnacles. "And this is just the start of my garden." Uncle smiled, both proud and pleased— like someone who knows a secret that you do not. "Too bad you don't want to see more of it."

I looked uncertainly at the cove. "You mean I have to swim?"

"Out there." He pointed to the reef that was exposed at low tide.

He was one shameless old man to tempt me that way and he knew it. I almost refused again, but I have to admit I was curious about that garden of his.

"Okay. I'll try just once more," I grumbled.

"We'll stay in the shallow end. Then, if you feel good, we can go out." Uncle walked farther into the water and half turned around as he took off his jacket. I whipped the towel off my shoulders and threw it high up on the beach. Uncle threw his jacket beside it. I waded into the sea until I was waist deep. I kept waiting for Uncle to shout instructions at me the way Dad would have, but he didn't.

I took a deep breath. Then another good one. Holding my arms ahead of me, I bent forward and kicked off from the sand. There was that shock for a moment of letting go of the land, and then I was floating. The cold water didn't feel so bad this time. I twisted my head to the side and breathed in the air and then slid over, floating on my back, letting the sun warm my face and skin.

Uncle began swimming in the water toward me. The spray from his splashing sent a drizzle over me, and then his body was floating alongside of me. He didn't shout anything at me or tell me how to do things better; he just warned me, "Careful. Don't go out too far."

So we stayed floating on our backs for a few minutes.

"Do you want to swim out to the reef?" I asked Uncle finally.

"Oh-kay." Uncle grinned. He started to move his arms, raising a glittering shower around his head as he swam out toward the rock reef. I followed him much more slowly and clumsily. Once Uncle was at the reef, he stretched out his arms and clung to a large boulder, hoisting himself up. He perched on the boulder with all the ease of a sea gull, as if he had done this thousands of times. I suppose he had if you thought about all the years he had spent in the cove.

Aware of Uncle watching me, I kept on churning toward the reef. I thought he might have some instructions for improvement by now, but still he didn't say anything.

Instead, he only reached out one hand. I clasped it and Uncle almost pulled me up out of the water to sit beside him—I mean, as if he were as rooted as a starfish to that boulder.

"What—?" I began.

"Shhh. Listen." Uncle swept his hand along, palm downward and parallel to the sea, in a short, sharp gesture for quiet.

At first, though, my main concern was getting a better grip on that big rock, but then as I sat there, I could feel the rhythm of the sea surging against the rocky reef that protected the cove, trying to make the opening in the reef bigger. The sea wasn't pounding so much as steadily pushing, as if it knew it had all the time in the world and could be patient. But after sitting there for a while, I almost felt like the reef was living and I could feel its heart beating.

Even now at low tide, I could feel the fine mist in the air—I suppose it was spray from the waves moving against the reef. But it felt almost like the breath of the rocks around me, breathing slowly and quietly along with the beating of the reef's heart.

"We'll start up there, boy." Uncle pointed toward the top of the reef.

"What about the big waves?" I was too interested to pay attention to the cold air.

Uncle shook his head. "I don't think there will be any more. And if there are, the reef will protect us." He patted a rock affectionately. Then he turned and began climbing. I followed him more cautiously the three feet or so to the top of the reef. I took one look at that big empty sea beyond the reef, and then I turned my head back in toward the cove.

Uncle waved his hand to indicate both sides of the reef. "When the sea goes out, all around here—maybe in little cracks, maybe on ledges—there are pools left. And the rocks, maybe they protect the pools so the big strong waves"—Uncle pantomimed a crashing wave stopped short—"the waves can't reach the pools. Then all kinds of things can grow." He spoke slowly and proudly, as if he were just about to pry up the lid to a treasure chest.

At that moment to my right—from a crevice I thought would be too small for anything to live in—a bright blue-and-purple crab scuttled out. It was only a few inches across. It paused when it saw us, and lifted its claws, ready to defend itself. Tiny bubbles frothed at its mouth.

Uncle reached across my lap to wiggle a finger above its head just out of the reach of its claws. The crab scuttled back into its crevice. "The brave, bold hero," Uncle said with a laugh. "Maybe when he goes home, he tells a lot of tales about fighting us." Carefully Uncle stood up then. He held out his hand, and I took it for support as I got slowly to my feet.

"Now do what I do." Confidently, Uncle turned his back to the sea and began to edge sideways along the top of the reef.

Uncle made it look real easy, but I found myself spreading my arms for better balance and I began to wish the rocks wouldn't vibrate. It was like walking on the back of some sleeping snake that might wake up and shake me off at any moment.

Uncle stopped where two rectangular slabs of rock leaned their tips against one another. One rock faced toward the sea, the other faced toward the cove. He waited shyly for me. I looked down between the rocks. There was a shallow depression on the giant boulder on which the two slabs rested. I caught my breath. The stone looked gray-black when it was wet, and the seawater was almost clear here; and in the daylight, the colors seemed even brighter. There were anemones of all colors—animals shaped like flowers, whose thin petals moved with a life of their own in the still water. Uncle leaned forward, supporting himself against the slabs. His hand barely stirred the surface of the pool as his finger brushed the petals of a red anemone. In the wink of an eye, the anemone had closed up, looking like a fat, bumpy doughnut. The other anemones closed up too. Uncle removed his hand from the pool. We waited for a little while until one by one they opened once again. They were all kinds of bright colors— orange, red, yellow, solid colors that would make any artist ache inside to be able to use.

Uncle paused where a flat slab of rock leaned against the top of the reef. He pointed inside. "Can you see it?"

I looked in at the shadows. It looked like a big ball of spines within the water under the slab. "What is it?"

"A sea urchin," Uncle explained. "It come up into the high tide pools."

Even as we watched, the sea urchin retreated farther into the shadows by moving its needlelike spines.

From there we climbed lower on the reef to the top of a small boulder which had crumbled. Uncle squatted down. I did the same.

Uncle waited, hands clasped, arms resting on top of his thighs. He looked like he could stay in that position forever. "There." Uncle pointed carefully to the shadow of a rock, at a sluglike thing with little stubby tubes at one end and the rest of its back covered with bright orange-red spots. It crept upside down across the pool as if the surface was a floor to it. Behind it, it left a little silver thread.

"He leaves a trail behind him. You know, like a land slug, that's his cousin. See that silver line? That's it. Watch what happens when I break it." Uncle reached down and touched the silvery thread behind the slug. The slug fell slowly through the water as if whatever invisible wires held it up had suddenly broken. When it landed gently on its back on the bottom of the pool, it slowly twisted about in the water, righting itself, and began crawling up the side again. "He keeps on trying, so I know he's gonna get cross."

Uncle stood up, wiping his hands on the sides of his swimming trunks. "You know all the pools around here. Well, some of them are big. Some of them are small. And every pool is cut off from the other. Maybe the pools are this far apart." Uncle held his hands an inch from each other. "But the pools, they might as well be miles and miles apart because the animal in one pool won't know about an animal in another pool. You take any animal around here and it would probably think its own pool is the whole world, and it doesn't know there are pools and pools all around it." Uncle sounded awed by the magic and vastness of what he owned.

The sea must have been rising higher because the waves were beginning to splash over the top of the reef. I hadn't noticed the narrow little channel before—it was really more like a scratch along the surface of the rocks. But the anemones' pool at the top of the reef must have begun to fill up, because a little trickle of water began to snake its way down into the pool of the sea urchin and then slipped down the channel again, rounded a corner, and slid in a curve down the surface of a rock, into the pool of the slug and on. So Uncle wasn't exactly right. There was a little thread of water connecting the tide pools sometimes before the sea did come in.

"I never dreamed there was so much to see," I said.

Uncle leaned forward and pretended to peer at something for emphasis. "You have to learn how to pay attention to things." He added, "But first you have to like yourself." He gave a tug to his trunks and sat down. "People who don't like themselves, they spend all their time looking at their faults. They don't have time to look at the world."

"What's there to like about myself?" I sat down and bent my knees so I could wrap my arms around my legs and lean my chest against my thighs. "I'm lousy at swimming. I'm lousy at all the *Westerners'* games. I'm lousy at making friends. I'm even lousy at being Chinese. I'm not like anything Dad wants."

Uncle raised one eyebrow. "Is that all you think your father wants? Play games all the time?"

I hugged my legs tighter against my chest. "That's all we ever do."

"Your father, he want other things too." Uncle ran a finger lightly over a scab on his thumb. "At least he used to. I remember when he was a small boy—smaller than you, maybe only ten or eleven. It was only talk from a small boy, but it was GOOD talk. He tell me, 'Uncle, I'm going to know everything about plants. You want to know something about them, you come to me.'" Uncle cocked his head to one side. "Your father always have some book about plants. Always so he can read from it when he have nothing else to do."

It was funny hearing about Dad when he was a small boy; but what Uncle told me helped explain why Dad had been so hot to start a garden on our very first day here. "I guess he still likes plants," I said.

Uncle, though, was too busy reminiscing to hear me. "And your father, when he wasn't reading or talking about plants, he was drawing them."

"That's a little hard to swallow," I said. I couldn't associate anything artistic with my dad—not even something like drawing wavy lines on a notepad while he was talking on the phone.

Uncle stiffened and he thrust out his chin. "I'm no liar. I got eyes. I saw them. Maybe the pictures aren't so good, but he say drawing the pictures teach him more than just reading about the plants."

"It's just that I never heard Dad say anything about drawing." I set my chin on top of my knees.

"Your father, he want to grow all kinds of plants and flowers." Uncle pounded his fist against the rock he was sitting on. His fist made a flat, slapping sound. "But your grandfather, he say no. He say it's a waste of money to buy flower seeds. Waste of time to grow them. Your grandfather only let your father grow some vegetables. And your grandfather, he get mad when he find all the drawings. Your grandfather say not to waste good paper that cost so much."

Uncle put his hands down on either side of him and leaned back. "And I watch what happen. Your father was a good boy. It was just like he close a door inside himself. No more books about plants. No more drawing. And," Uncle added sadly, "no more talk about knowing everything about plants. He even tell me he not care about that stuff. But I got eyes. I saw."

I bit my lip for a moment and stared at the sea. It was a sad-enough sounding story—whether it was true or not. I guess I could believe some of what Uncle had said—at least the part about Dad's once wanting to grow some flowers, because it would help explain why he had already been planning a garden on our very first day at the store.

It also helped explain his determination to try after the cats had ruined his first plantings. He said he was going to show those cats just who actually ran that backyard. As soon as we could qualify, Dad had taken me to the library to get a card—or so he said—but he'd gotten a card for himself as well. The cards were only temporary cards at first, so we could take out only two books each. Even so, Dad had headed straight for the gardening books like he had memorized their location, and he had taken out two gardening books and talked me into taking out two more. And when we had finally gotten our real cards and could take out six books on each card, Dad had taken out more gardening books.

Finally last month, in March, when Dad had devoured all the gardening books on the library shelves, he had gone to the gardening store and come back with little boxes of flowers to be transplanted. The flowers, Dad informed us, were already large enough to survive the cats and hardy enough to like shady places the best.

Dad had felt so triumphant when he could show us the first flower bud. It was no bigger than my fingernail and colored lavender. Mom was pleased because Dad was happy, and I said something about how pretty it looked, but in that gray gloomy backyard the flower bud—I forgot the name of the flower—seemed small and insignificant, and even the color didn't seem very bright.

But that didn't seem to stop Dad's enthusiasm as each new bud appeared until there were a lot of them; and that was nothing compared to the time when the first bud began to flower. It was really only half open, with the petals still partly upright, but Dad had pantomimed the opening of the flower with his fingers like he could already see it. I thought Dad had been so happy because he had managed to beat the cats at their own game. Now I could see that the flowers meant more to him.

I looked at Uncle. "Why was Grandfather so mean?"

"All the money have to go home to China. To the wife and the rest of the family there." Uncle shrugged like it was an old story.

"Not even a little something for Dad?" I wondered. There was a little part inside me that began to feel sorry for Dad.

"The family," Uncle explained simply, "always comes first." He said it as if that should be explanation enough—as if I should already have known that. But Uncle might as well have been talking about the families of people on Jupiter, because it sounded so strange to me.

"That's when your father find other things." Uncle leaned over toward me. "He get real good then at *demon* games. See, not all the old-timers think *demon* games are waste of time. Some of the clubs in different Chinatowns, they have teams. Your grandfather, he grumble a little, but he like the respect he get because of your father." Uncle slapped my leg with the back of his hand. "The other Chinese tell your grandfather he must be one strong, quick man if he have a son that strong and that quick. So as long as your father get good grades in school and work hard in the store, he can play the different games. But you remember that the *demon* games"—Uncle tilted his head up—"they were always your father's second choice."

"I still wish," I said, "that I could be as good as my dad."

Uncle sighed and shook his head. "You try too hard to be Calvin's son." He seemed dissatisfied with what he had said—as if he didn't have enough English to explain all his thoughts to me and he knew I didn't know enough Chinese if we used that language. Uncle folded his legs into a lotus position as if he wanted to become more comfortable before he stretched his arm out toward me. "It's not good if you do everything just like your father. Everyone is different. That's what makes them special." Uncle waved his hand grandly to include the entire reef. "You think it good if all the animals look the same, hah?"

"I have to keep on trying." I shrugged my shoulders, annoyed with Uncle for being so insistent.

There was a long silence while we both listened to the ocean beating against his reef. Finally, I said, "Dad has flower boxes." I thought Uncle might like to know. "He works there every day."

Uncle smiled slowly and nodded his head in approval. "Good. I'm glad Calvin finally got his flowers."

He glanced up at the top of the reef. We could see the spray rising in the air. The drizzle in the air was changing to more like a shower. "Maybe we should go back now," Uncle said. "This reef's not a good place when the tide rises."

"Can't we stay a little while longer?"

"Oh-kay. Oh-kay. A little while then," Uncle said indulgently. I leaned back to look up at the broad sweep of sky overhead. Somehow, sitting on the reef, I felt like the world was a much bigger place than it seemed when I was standing on solid ground. And so much of what I knew when I was on the land didn't seem as certain anymore. I couldn't help hunching my shoulders a little.

Uncle must have been observing me. "Back to the beach, boy. Look at you. You're shivering."

"Not at the cold. It's—"

"No arguments. Come on." Uncle slipped off the rocks into the water.

When we were back on the beach again, I began to shiver for real. A strong wind had begun to sweep in from the sea, so that it was a lot colder than when we had first swum out to the reef. I got my towel from where I had thrown it on the beach and came back toward Uncle, rubbing at my arms and back vigorously.

Uncle did not bother to towel himself. He had rolled around in the sand until he had a thin film covering him. Then he had put on his jacket and sprawled out on the beach to soak up what sun there was.

"Where did you learn how to swim so good?" I sat down beside him.

Uncle turned his head to look at me. "Don't you think we got water in China?"

"You know what I mean." I shrugged my arms through the sleeves of my shirt.

Uncle smiled. "I come from China when I was small. Very small. And I was raised here. Over in the China Camp near Monterey. There used to be a whole bunch of us catching fish there. My father, he was smart. So the others had him speak to *the white demons*. He learned their language pretty good and he taught me. That's how come I speak American so good." Uncle swept his arms out from his sides and then back down, so that he began to dig shallow depressions in the sand that looked like wings. "You know, a long, long time ago, *the T'ang people*, they call San Francisco the Big City. Sacramento is the Little City. And you know all the tide pools on the reef? Well, I bet there were just as many Chinatowns in this state."

"What happened to them all?" I began to towel off my legs.

Uncle lifted his head and cleared his throat. "One day the sea go out and it never come back, and the pools, they all dry up. And my father and me and some others, we come here."

I spread my towel over my legs like a blanket. "What do you mean?"

"Never mind, boy." He laid his head back down on the sand and stared up at the sky. "Young people, what do they care what happened a long time ago?"

I looked at Uncle. He'd set his jaw firmly like there wasn't any room for argument. "Does anyone visit you?"

"Oh, the older ones in my family, they used to visit." Uncle grasped a handful of sand. "But maybe they're too old now. Maybe they don't like to drive the long way from the City. And the younger ones, they don't remember. They forget about the fun they have swimming here. Even some I teach how to swim." He flung the sand into the air and watched the wind scatter it along the beach. He said as if it were the deadliest insult, "They prefer the tame water in those concrete ponds in their own backyards. They turn their faces from the sea and the things I show them." He added, "Even your father."

I tucked the towel around my legs. "Did you take my father diving for abalone as well?"

"Sure," Uncle said.

"When can I go?" I asked him.

Uncle scratched his cheek for a moment as if he were feeling uncomfortable. "I got to give you real special training to go diving. Not everyone can dive."

"Then when can we start?" I asked impatiently.

"You don't even swim so good. You swim better. Then we can begin your training." Uncle slapped his hands at an imaginary surface. "You still fight the water too much. You must use the sea and you must let it use you."

"But how can I learn to swim better so I can be trained?" I rubbed the back of my neck in annoyance. "You never tell me what to do."

Uncle blinked his eyes, puzzled. "You learn from inside you." He tapped at his heart. "Not from outside. And not from some old man's big mouth."

I'd take Uncle's method of teaching me any day over Dad's way. "So when do you think I'll be ready?"

Uncle folded his arms across his chest and leaned forward so that his forearms rested on top of his drawn-up knees. "You gotta be comfortable in the water. I can't say."

So maybe his cove wasn't a perfect place. It was still special. For all of his quirks, Uncle still managed to make me feel like a real person. "I wish I could stay here."

Uncle was so surprised that he couldn't completely hide his pleasure. "Well, you can't, *little demon*. But you can come here next Saturday." He wagged his finger at me. "And remember. Don't tell anyone about what I teach you."

"Sure," I said breezily. At the time, the promise seemed like an easy thing to keep. I didn't realize what would happen when I broke that promise.

CHAPTER | V

I

When I left the cove, I found Kenyon sitting by the path with a long-stemmed weed in her hand. She twitched it up and down, teasing the heads of the other weeds around her. I think Kenyon was probably the sharpest kid in our class, even though she didn't do all that well in school because she rarely did her homework. She was curious about everything, so I wasn't all that surprised to see her here.

"Did you have fun?" she asked.

I wound the chain around the gatepost and then through the gate. "You saw us?" I asked cautiously.

"Oh, I come by here every now and then to take a look." She slipped the stem of the weed between her teeth. "Padlocks always get to me. I always want to know what's being kept out. Or kept in."

I took the padlock from where it hung on the mesh and locked it through the links of the chain. "How long have you been spying on us?"

"A few minutes. But I can't hear too well from up here."

"That's too bad," I said sarcastically.

Kenyon pulled the weed from between her teeth. "What were you guys looking at on the reef?"

"Nothing that'd interest you."

"I don't know." She lifted the weed over her shoulder like it was a spear and threw it away. "I like a lot of different things." She didn't look very tough at that moment. In fact she sounded almost wistful when she added, "You're lucky to have a friend that owns his own private beach. It looks so peaceful down there."

"It is, and I'd like it to stay that way. It's a special place." I pointed toward the long curve of the public beach that swept for miles around the bay. "You can go swimming anytime you like. Why do you have to ruin this?"

"How could I do that?" Kenyon asked in innocent surprise—as if she had never said a mean word to make me miserable all these months.

"You'll make fun of my uncle just like you make fun of me."

"Make fun?" Kenyon was wearing a floppy suede hat with a shapeless crown and a wide brim that kept flapping in her face. "There's one thing you have to understand about me. I'm a cranky person and I expect other people to be just as cranky or get out of my way." She held up her hat brim. "I kept waiting and waiting for you to say something back. But you never did. You just took it and then the others picked it up and it kinda got out of hand."

"Things got way out of hand." I started past her. I heard her get up and hurry to catch up with me.

"I never meant anything by it," she said. "Honest. It's just that I found out when I was real small that if I didn't zap the other kids real quick, they'd start on my folks."

"Are your folks very different?"

Kenyon rolled her eyes. "Craigles, my boy, you don't know the half of it. Anyway, zapping the kids has got so that it's a habit with me. . . . I mean, I know how easy it is to make them laugh and they kinda expect me to make them laugh."

We walked down the path and across the beach parking lot. I kept on thinking about what Kenyon had said so I could figure out how she was trying to trick me, but she seemed to be being honest and open with me at that moment. Like she'd taken off all her prickly armor for once.

Funny, but I guess Uncle was right. I mean, there's a lot more to the world and especially to people than I thought. And people can be just like those animals in the tide pools—the pools can be only inches apart and yet the animals are almost in separate worlds. The moment I realized that, I knew that I didn't want to be like some animal that was stuck in its own pool. "Why are you telling me all this?" I asked. I paused by the Coast Road and looked to either side.

She held the brim of her hat up against the crown so it wouldn't cover her eyes. "I thought that . . . well, maybe once we understood one another, maybe I could go swimming in the cove. I got this kind of bug in me. I mean, the more someone keeps me from doing something, the more I gotta do it."

I looked at her coldly. "Is that all you want? The gate was unlocked. You could have pushed your way into the cove anytime." The road was clear so I crossed.

Kenyon followed me. "I don't go where I haven't been invited."

"Well, I don't decide who swims in the cove." I picked up my pace so I could walk away from her quickly. The wagon rattled loudly behind me.

"But you could put in a good word for me." Kenyon caught up with me again along the dirt road. Ahead of us I could see the neat little beach cottages of Mrs. Koch.

I would have to find some other excuse to put her off. I shook my head. "Uncle's kinda cranky and shy. It was all I could do to get him to talk to me."

"He can't be any funnier than either of my folks." Kenyon draped her sweater over her back and began to tie the sleeves in a big knot just under her neck.

"Maybe." I concentrated on pulling the wagon along.

"You just think I'm putting you on, but I mean it." Kenyon wagged one of the sleeves up and down for a moment. "God, you don't know how I had to fight for this. Half the time Dory just hands her old work shirts and coats to me even if they're covered with clay from her pots."

I guessed that Dory was her mother. "She makes pots?"

Kenyon nodded. "Sometimes you can see her wading in Concepcion Creek. She's getting clay from the banks to use for her pots."

I glanced at Kenyon curiously. "Why doesn't she just buy some clay from a store?"

"Really." Kenyon sniffed disdainfully. "You're so booj-wah."

"What's that?" I asked suspiciously.

"B-o-u-r-g-e-o-i-s. It's French for what Dory and Archie aren't, aren't, aren't. And it's what they say I am." She picked at the sleeve, straightening out a fold there. "Dory can't see why I don't want to go through my life like I just escaped from a carnival."

"Some of your things are kind of nice." I was only trying to make her feel better, but I only seemed to make her angrier.

"If you're a gypsy," she snapped. "She spends half her time in the secondhand stores buying old army jackets or old-time dresses with lace that's falling off. She always says she's going to fix it. Ha!"

"She probably doesn't have all that much time with all the work she has to do."

Kenyon bit her lip. "It isn't like that. I mean, it's what she says to me." Kenyon hunched her shoulders together and held her arms in tight against her sides, so that when she gestured wildly it was only with her forearms. Her voice went up high and sounded all fluttery and excited. I supposed she was imitating her mother. "'Really, Kenyon. Really. You're always into Things, dear. But Things aren't important.'" Kenyon thrust one arm out stiffly. "'Do be a dear now and hand me my Gole-wahz.'"

"What's that?"

Kenyon raised one arm and bent her wrist languidly as she pretended to take a puff from something. "French cigarettes that are so strong they smell like burnt camels. The only people I know who smoke them are French sailors and Dory. Only Dory can't usually afford them. All she can afford are American cigarettes."

"How do you know about French sailors?" I asked, fascinated.

Despite herself, Kenyon seemed pleased. "We went to France." She went into her breathless, fluttery imitation of her mother again. "'Frah-nce is the ONLY civilized nation.'" She shrugged and became herself again. "We went there two years ago when Dory inherited a little money, and we came back when we'd gone through most of it."

I couldn't help smiling excitedly. "You're the only person I've ever met who's been to France. I mean that sounds so fantastic."

"Then you haven't heard Archie talk." She put her hands to the knot that she had made with the sleeves of her sweater.

"Is Archie your dad?" We had reached the sidewalk by then.

"Yeah." Nervously she pulled at her sleeves, making the knot tighter. "He and Dory split up three years ago. He still comes over a lot though. Mostly they argue about who's less 'booj-wah' than the other."

"You're just exaggerating." I waved a hand at her. "Nobody acts like that."

My words only seemed to infuriate Kenyon. "The hell they don't. Archie didn't even want us to go to Europe. He said the whole idea was so antiquated that it wasn't even 'booj-wah.' We ought to go to India instead. Archie kept on saying that India was the mother of all nations." Kenyon gave a twisted little smile. "I told Archie he was a crock of shit."

I just stopped where I was on the sidewalk and stared at Kenyon. "I don't believe you said that to your father."

She threw back her head defiantly. "Well, I did. And if he was around right now, I'd say it to him again."

"Just to show me? You're crazy." I tried to start walking again, but the wagon wouldn't budge. I turned to see Kenyon with her foot blocking one of the rear wheels.

"I call Archie that, or a lot of worse things," Kenyon insisted. "Old Archie isn't into being a fascist."

"A what?" I gave a tug and the wagon began to roll over her foot, so Kenyon snatched her foot back just before the wagon went completely over it.

"You know." She turned sideways, skipping along as she kept pace with me. "Like a Hitler or a Mussolini. Anyway, Archie never does anything to me. And he usually doesn't say anything to me right away. He just sends me a poem a week later." She said the word "poem" with a sarcastic grimace like she was chewing on old leather.

"Well, not many parents make up poems for their children." I kept trying to find the bright side of things, but Kenyon seemed to want to keep dragging things back under the rock.

"The poem wasn't FOR me, it was ABOUT me," Kenyon corrected me. She half closed her eyes and began to recite in a deep, singsong voice.

> *"The squirrel's going to her plasterboard tree*
> *With the desk and bureau and bed from Sears*
> *To open up her empty plastic Easter eggs. . . ."*

She opened her eyes. "You get the picture. I told him that the next poem he sent me had to rhyme, but he didn't do it. He still won't."

"Rhyme isn't the important thing." I knew that much at least. "I mean, maybe he was trying to tell you something in the poem that he couldn't tell you face to face."

"Archie?" She shook her head. "He's past trying to tell stuff to people. He's now into the dark armpit of despair." A breeze swept down the street suddenly and Kenyon put a hand to the top of her hat to hold it down. "I mean, I just want to be like everybody else, only Dory and Archie keep saying that no one is like anybody else so I just better grin and bear it."

I had to laugh. "I can't see you being like Sheila."

Kenyon leaned her head toward me and said in a low, conspiratorial voice, "I suppose not. She listens to David Cassidy records. She must have bubbles on the brain by now."

"Well, you see, it's just as well that your parents are right." I smiled because it was what Uncle had said too.

Kenyon frowned and shook her head slowly. She turned so she was again walking in the direction we were facing. "Oh, you are one sad case, all right. Look, Craigles. When Dory or Archie tells me that we're all different, it's just an excuse for one of them—it depends on whose house I'm staying at—to shove me out the door and go find myself. It's their polite way of saying, 'Don't bother me, kid, while I'm working.'"

"Yeah, well, I guess they're artists, after all." I put

both hands behind me to grip the handle of the wagon.

"Bullshit." Kenyon folded her arms and stared moodily at her worn sneakers. "They didn't want a kid, they wanted an answering service. When I'm at Archie's I take the phone calls for poetry readings, and when I'm at Dory's I answer the door and show the boutique people where to pick up the neo-Aztec ashtrays they've bought from her."

In her own way, Kenyon wanted sympathy. I should have kept my mouth shut, but I couldn't help asking skeptically, "How do you do all that if one of them shoves you out the door like you say they do?"

Kenyon took her hat off for a moment while she smoothed some stray strands of hairs from her eyes. "I sit on the doorstep, stupid. Dory and Archie couldn't put one of those metal jockeys on their front lawn, so they had me to put there instead. And when they split up, one of them takes me every other month." She jammed her hat back on her head and smiled insolently. "Thought you had me, didn't you?"

When Kenyon spoke, it was hard to tell what was fact and what was fiction because she was always trying to make you laugh—and maybe feel sorry for her at the same time. Even so, I found myself liking her. "Do you feel like a Pepsi?"

Kenyon grinned. "Do I? Dory and Archie just hate that rotgut." Kenyon threw up her hands in mock horror and did her imitation of her mother. "'Think of all that carbonated sugar water, Kenyon. And the dyes. And the preservatives. It's so . . . so unhealthy.'" Kenyon pretended to give a delicate little shudder and then she spoke in her normal voice. "And Dory says that all to me while she's chain-smoking."

"A carton and a half a week." I nodded my head. I smiled at Kenyon. "The people in a grocery store know a lot about their customers."

"Hey, look, Craigles, before we go any further, what's wrapped up in all that newspaper anyway?" Kenyon pointed behind us at the wagon.

"Uncle's garbage," I said reluctantly. "Mostly tin cans that he washes out so they don't smell. Stuff like that." I tensed, waiting for Kenyon to say something about Uncle.

"Garbage, hunh? I remember the time Dory was big on recycling stuff. That was about the time we came back from France and were dead broke." She spoke in a high voice. "'Oh, Kenyon, we simply mustn't waste our resources.'" Kenyon dropped her voice back to normal. "Mostly it was an excuse for Dory to go around getting the old cigarette butts from the ashtrays and tearing up the tobacco so she could roll her own cigarettes."

"Sure," I said skeptically again.

We walked past the old Chinese standing about in front of their hotel and smoking while they read the pages of the newspaper that belonged to the hotel. Kenyon sniffed appreciatively at the odor of frying meat coming from the cafe, and I didn't have the heart to warn her that most of the food in there was pure poison. I found, though, that I liked Kenyon. She wasn't one of those bothersome people who ask a question every minute. She seemed to be taking everything in so she could think about it before she asked any questions—if she ever did. The old Chinese pointedly ignored Kenyon, in her floppy hat and jeans. They seemed determined sometimes never to show surprise at what Americans or American-born Chinese did.

Mom greeted Kenyon in her friendly way, and Kenyon wouldn't take more than a Pepsi. She had to refuse, in turn, a Fudgsicle, some freshly cut, wine-soaked salami, and some Chinese almond cookies. Uncle Lester usually brought a box down from the City when he came to check on his store, so he must have just paid a visit to Mom and Dad.

"How do you know you won't like them if you won't try them?" Mom held the scissors against the thin red string wound round the pink box.

Kenyon clasped her Pepsi bottle, one hand above the other. "Oh, I've tried them at the Celestial Garden."

"You eat at the expensive places." Mom tried to laugh. "What are they doing serving almond cookies with dinner?"

"We asked for dessert." Kenyon looked first at Mom and then at me. "Aren't you supposed to?" She took a drink from her Pepsi.

"Not really," I said.

Kenyon took the bottle from her mouth. A little Pepsi splashed on her upper lip and she wiped her face with her fingers. "Sometimes dessert's the best part of a meal."

"All those fancy dishes and you liked dessert instead?" Mom asked. "What did you have?"

"Let's see." Kenyon scratched absently at her forehead. "I don't know the Chinese names. But I think we had shark's fin soup—are they really sharks' fins?—and pressed duck and some squiggly things. Do you know how to make that kind of stuff?"

"Me?" Mom pressed her fingers below her throat and laughed. "No, I cook American mostly, or maybe plain Chinese style. You know, chop up meat and stuff big mushrooms and steam cook them."

"Outasight," Kenyon said enthusiastically.

"Well, maybe you can come to dinner one night." Mom smiled at her pleasantly. "Did you like Chinatown up in the City?"

Kenyon took another sip from her Pepsi. "The stores were great."

Mom got to reminiscing with Kenyon about Grant Avenue for a long time. Even if Kenyon couldn't remember the names of the stores, Mom could describe some of them in enough detail for Kenyon to recognize them. Among her other jobs, Mom had worked in a souvenir store as a clerk; and even if she hadn't liked her job much at that time, she now seemed to enjoy remembering the Chinatown stores. I think Mom missed Chinatown almost as much as I did.

Finally, Kenyon glanced at the Hires root beer clock on our wall and said she had to go.

"Aren't you going to stay for dinner?" Mom asked.

"Thank you very much," Kenyon said politely. "But Archie's coming over and me and him and Dory are going over to Santa Cruz. We're going to see DUCK SOUP. The university's having a Marx Brothers festival." She finished the rest of her Pepsi and set the empty bottle down on top of the counter.

"I heard it's a good movie." Mom took the bottle

and set it in the cardboard box with the other empties.

"Why don't you come along with us?" Kenyon looked first at Mom and then at Dad. "Ms. Chin? Mr. Chin?"

Dad hadn't spoken to Kenyon in all this time. He was like one of the anemones in that pool that closed up the moment something large and new entered the pool. Now he gave a little nervous laugh. "I don't know. My wife gets pretty tired after work."

Mom dug her elbow into Dad's side. "Oh, you're the one who gets really tired. You're the one who would probably be snoring in the movie." Dad didn't say anything. Embarrassed, he moved away, rubbing his side.

Kenyon turned around in the doorway and held up one hand, wriggling her fingers. "Well, 'bye. Thanks for everything." Mom and Dad smiled again and nodded.

When I came back from throwing away Uncle's garbage, Dad was putting some bottles of Thunderbird wine into the refrigerator.

"She's very nice," Mom said. "Very—um—self-possessed."

Dad put in a bottle of red Ripple wine. "Yes, she is." He said it in a very matter-of-fact way, as if he really were concentrating on something else.

I picked up some of the bottles of white Ripple from the top of the ice-cream freezer, which was next to the refrigerator. "I'll do that, Dad."

"You took long enough." Dad stepped back to let me by. "Did you go over to the school yard to play a game?"

"No, sir. I visited Uncle."

Dad raised his eyebrows. "Why didn't you find the other guys and get a game going?"

I put the bottles in carefully between the row of Thunderbird and the row of red Ripple. "I just didn't feel like it, Dad." I turned and got the other two white Ripple bottles from the freezer top.

"A boy who sits around all day talking to old men and girls instead of playing with the guys"—Dad shook his head—"that boy is a funny kid."

I didn't answer Dad. I didn't trust myself to say anything because I felt so mad. This afternoon with Kenyon and Uncle had made me feel good for one of the few times since we had moved down here, and now Dad was calling it ridiculous. I just went around behind the counter. My steps sounded loud on the long, thin wooden planks we kept on the concrete floor to cut down on the chill. I began to take the empty soda bottles out of the cardboard box where we put the bottles that had been returned for a refund.

Dad leaned his stomach against the counter and tapped his fingers on the glass top. "You want to practice some dribbling?"

"No, sir." I got some small satisfaction from saying that. "I think I better sort out some of these empties now."

Mom had gone over to the bins where we kept the vegetables. She had begun to tear the old leaves from the heads of lettuce. Mom wouldn't look at me. She obviously thought I should have spent more time with Dad.

Dad joined me behind the counter. "Come on," he coaxed.

"No thank you," I mumbled. I wasn't going to let Dad ruin this afternoon any more than he had already. The last thing I needed was to have him shout at me during a basketball practice.

"Humph, you'd rather spend your time talking to old men and girls." Dad repeated himself contemptuously. He wanted to make it clear that real all-American boys didn't do that. He slid around me and got a chicken and cleaver and took them into the back room to work in the sink. I suppose he was going to cut it up for a customer. None of us—not me, not Dad, not Mom—said anything for a while. Each of us had closed up like an anemone. I thought of what Uncle had told me about Dad—about how Dad had wanted to learn about plants and how my grandfather made him give up that dream.

If it was true, I didn't want to be the one to force him to shut off another dream.

I felt so bad that after I had cleared out about half the empties from the box, I went into the back room where Dad was pounding away at the chicken with his cleaver. "Dad," I said. He didn't hear me at first because of the noise from the chopping. I raised my voice. "Dad?"

Dad turned. "What is it, boy?"

I pointed toward the counter. "I made enough room now for more empties. You want to try and dribble some?"

Dad wouldn't admit that it was he who really wanted me to dribble the basketball. He wiped his hands on a towel. "If you want to."

The practice went like it usually did: lousy. But then the basketball happened to bounce on top of one of the wooden soda-pop crates that Dad was using as a flower box. "Hey." Dad rushed over to the box. "You'll crush your mom's flowers." Impatiently he began to inspect the primroses. He'd gotten them as small plants from a garden supply store and transplanted them into the box. They were just blooming now.

Watching Dad work on his flowers, I thought I saw a chance to find out if Uncle had really been telling the truth about when Dad was small. I was kind of hoping that he had, because then Dad could tell me about how much he had wanted to grow some flowers; and maybe then I could tell him just how much I sympathized with him—he could have been allowed to plant a few seeds at least. I thought we could become closer in a way that we never could throwing a stupid basketball through a hoop.

I picked up the basketball and rested it on my hip. "You really like gardening, don't you, Dad?" I asked conversationally.

"They're your mom's flowers." Dad picked up a trowel. "It's just that your mom hates bugs so I do this stuff for her."

I scratched my forehead, feeling annoyed with Dad. You didn't have to be a genius to see how much pleasure the garden gave him, but he seemed determined to deny that fact. "But," I protested, "you must like it a little. And Uncle claimed that you used to be really interested in plants when you were a kid."

My words seemed only to annoy Dad even more. He stuck the trowel point first in the dirt and turned, clapping his hands and holding them open. He wanted me to pass the basketball to him. "Just forget about Uncle," he instructed me.

I had been so eager to find something to share with

Dad besides basketball that I had forgotten what else Uncle had said. I mean, he had told me that when Dad had given up his dream of having his own small garden, he wouldn't talk about it. Uncle had said it was as if Dad had closed a door inside himself. I was getting the feeling now that Dad had not only shut the door, he'd locked and bolted it too.

I should have kept quiet right then, but instead I decided to keep pushing at that door. I mean so many of my "heart-to-heart" conversations with Dad sounded like rehashes of the sports page that I wanted to talk about something that really meant something—like when Dad had been small.

I waved my hand vaguely around the garden. "I was just wondering why you took so much trouble with all of this. I thought you made the garden because you couldn't have one when you were a kid." I meant my words in a kindly way, just like everything else I had said during the practice.

But Dad just wouldn't share his boyhood experiences with me. Maybe he didn't want to talk about the past because he would also have had to remember all the hurt and frustration he had felt. If he had just said something like that, I could have understood. In fact I would have accepted any excuse really. But it was as if

Dad didn't want to admit even that much. Instead, Dad put all the blame on me. "Don't stall our practice with all this stupid talk."

"I'm not stalling," I protested. "I really want to know about when you were a kid."

"You're just being lazy. No one cares about those days."

I felt so frustrated with Dad that I became angry myself. I balanced the basketball between the fingertips of both my hands. "Maybe we should just forget the practice."

Dad reached a hand inside his shirt and scratched his shoulder. "Hey, I didn't ask you to come out here. You asked me, remember?"

I'd started out this practice with the best intentions of getting closer to Dad. Instead, I'd only managed to make him angry. I thought again of my promise to Mom. I had to make Dad think he was doing a good job.

"You're right, Dad. I'm sorry. Let's work on my dribbling." I began bouncing the ball against the concrete.

But Dad jammed his hands into his pockets. "You sure that's what you want?"

"Yeah. Really." I tried to sound as sincere as I could.

He gave a sullen little toss of his head. "Well, okay."

It was the worst practice I had ever had with Dad.

This time he didn't shout instructions. He just shrugged whenever I asked him about something and continued to watch me with the same dogged, sullen look.

So maybe it hurts to be all closed up like an anemone. But if I learned anything from that practice, it was that it sometimes hurt even worse to open up to other people. I don't know: Dad and I just didn't seem to be on the same wavelength. He misunderstood everything I tried to say and do.

II

But I wasn't the only one who had trouble with a parent. Kenyon did too; and it was like and yet unlike the trouble I was having with Dad, because Kenyon's father was a poet and not a basketball player. Her father came to visit our school that Monday. He said he built poems out of words the way someone else would use sticks to make a chair. All that would have sounded okay, except for the fact that he was wearing a long white robe and while he recited his poems, he shook something called a sistrum. He said it was a very old musical instrument, but it just looked like a metal frame with a lot of metal rods on it that jingled when he shook it.

Kenyon had gone out of her way to dress in her pink sweater, a white blouse, and a red polyester skirt. It was almost like she wanted to lose herself among the other girls in the class. All the time that her father was performing, reciting his poems in a high singsong chant and shaking his sistrum, Kenyon looked like she was ready to die of embarrassment.

"Now this is my idea of spring," her father said. He threw back his head and gave a quick shake to his sistrum and almost sang, "Pictures of myself on the pond. Blossoms fall and I am lost." He looked around. "Now what do you think I meant by that?" He glanced at Kenyon for help. It was funny, but Kenyon's dad had the same expression as Dad had whenever he was trying to coax me into shooting a few baskets.

But Kenyon sat slumped in her desk, looking sullen and almost angry, her arms folded across her stomach, and looking like she wished she was a thousand miles away.

Her dad raised his eyes toward heaven resignedly. He looked around the room and shook his sistrum nervously. He tried to sound cheerful. "Nobody wants to guess, hunh? Well, it's about springtime. I see my reflection floating on the surface of a pond and then some blossoms fall from the tree and they send ripples over the surface so that my reflection disappears. But what else do you think it's about?" When no one volunteered anything, he explained everything himself. "You see, it's also about our life here." He pointed his sistrum almost desperately at our teacher. "Now Mr. Loeb and I are going to pass out paper and pencils. I want you to draw something you see or do in the springtime."

He helped Mr. Loeb distribute everything and then Kenyon's dad went up and down the aisles, his flowing robe brushing the kids sometimes. He stood over me for a little while looking down on what I was drawing. I tried to pretend he wasn't near me. I heard him grunt and then he went on. In fifteen minutes I'd only begun my picture when he told us to stop drawing. Then he told us to turn the picture over and try to describe what we were trying to draw. Some of the others spent a long time but I finished quickly. I sat back in my desk, folding my arms.

Fifteen minutes went by on the classroom clock before he told us to stop writing. Then he asked for volunteers to read their stuff. When no one raised a hand, he nodded to Sheila and asked her to share her poem with the class. Sheila's voice was very shrill as if she were nervous. She read a short description of the pretty flowers in May.

"Very nice. That could be a good poem," he said mechanically, and then he nodded to me. "And you, you had an interesting picture."

"It's not so interesting." I could feel my ears turning red. I couldn't draw very well so I didn't want to show my drawing to the rest of the class.

"Please share it with us though."

Embarrassed, I concentrated on my paper, trying to ignore the others in the room. I began to read slowly, "See, in the springtime the tourists always come and you can never ride the cable cars."

"Good." He laughed and waved a hand at me. "Does everybody see? Springtime doesn't have to be the cruelest season of the year. It could be a funny poem."

Kenyon thrust her hand into the air. "I'd like to read mine."

"If you must." Kenyon's dad pretended to sigh and shrug his shoulders reluctantly, but actually he seemed rather pleased with his daughter.

Kenyon got out of her desk. She closed her eyes and threw back her head, reciting in the deep singsong voice her father had used when reciting his poems. "The daisies that bloom in the grass, alas/Are all being crushed by some poet's fat ass." She sat down quickly.

Her father winced and sighed as if he had to go through this all the time. He forced himself to smile in the stunned silence. "A funny poem and it rhymes too."

He looked like he wanted to scold her but wasn't about to show her that she had managed to shock him.

"I've got a poem about a man who ate a toad and got warts on his tongue." Kenyon smiled brightly.

"No, no, it wouldn't be fair to the others to take up all the time," her father said weakly. He pointed quickly to someone else. "How about you? Would you describe your drawing?"

He left after a while, and then we did a little more schoolwork before the day ended. I thought Kenyon's dad took her joke really well. My dad would have shouted at me to give him more respect and then gone into a long sulk if I had done something like that to him. I wanted to tell her how much I had liked her dad; but when the final bell rang, Kenyon was the first one out of the door and heading for home.

Some of the guys tried to kid her about her dad, and she swung her book bag at them. Jim threw up his arm protectively and managed to knock it away, but he rubbed his arm and studied it to see if there was a bruise on it. And then Mr. Loeb had come out and the guys moved away from Kenyon, who was standing there swinging her book bag back and forth ready to hit someone else.

I picked up Kenyon's social studies book from where

it had landed after it had gone flying from her bag. I was going to give it to her, but Sheila grabbed my arm. For once, blood was thicker than water with Sheila.

"Geez, don't go near her. She's teed off enough now. I'll give it to her." Sheila took the book from me.

I tried to figure out just what kind of trick Sheila was playing on me. "What would she be mad about?" I asked suspiciously.

Sheila sighed in exasperation at my slowness. "Her dad comes to school once a year and she's always like this. Last year she got suspended for fighting after her dad's visit."

I looked after Kenyon. With her book bag slung over her shoulder ready to be swung at someone, she picked up her stride along the street. Funny, but she reminded me of the sea urchin Uncle had shown me. I mean, even if something or someone got into its tide pool, the sea urchin was so spiny that it let nothing get close to it. Though she was one of the most popular kids in school and I was one of the least, I found myself actually feeling sorry for Kenyon.

CHAPTER | VI

I

On Wednesday morning, after I had gotten dressed in the dark, I tried to put the bed away into the sofa quietly so I wouldn't wake up Mom and Dad. Then, as silently as I could, I went down the back steps from our flat above the store to the backyard. I slid the bar back from the backyard gate to wait in front of the store.

It was cold outside. Up at the intersection near the flophouse, I could see the men—mostly American or Chicano, but a few Chinese too—huddling around in small groups, their shoulders hunched together, hands thrust into their old pants or clutching the lapels of their coats, trying to pull them tighter about their necks against the morning cold. They were waiting to be hired to go into the fields to pick whatever was in season.

I was waiting for the morning papers. If someone didn't bring them in, the papers were likely to get ripped off. Eddy drove by in his blue-and-yellow truck and came to a screeching halt. He bent over, picked up a pile of newspapers, and tossed them down on the sidewalk. "Hi, kid," he called to me. "Happy reading." Then he jumped back onto the seat and, after giving the steering wheel a twist, roared away down the street.

I got out the key to the padlock on the gate that opened into the alleyway on the side of the store. I dragged the newspapers down the alley and into the back of the store, where we could open the stack and put them on the newspaper racks later. I was just relocking the padlock on the back gate when I saw this giant eight-foot-high rabbit stagger by. It wasn't really a giant rabbit. It was this cardboard cutout about six feet long and painted a bright purple and orange. Whoever was carrying it must have been stretching as far as he or she could, because I could see the fingertips on either side of the cutout.

At first I was going to go back inside, but my curiosity got the better of me. I waited for a pickup truck to rattle on by. A chicken feather floated out of the back. I tried to catch it as I crossed the street, but I missed.

"Hey, need some help?" I asked the rabbit.

The rabbit was slowly lowered to the sidewalk and I saw Kenyon. Underneath a blue cloth coat she wore a black nylon dress with some kind of Russian peasant design on it in orange flowers that looked pretty nice. She put her hands to the back of her neck and twisted her head first one way and then the other. "Morning."

I ran my finger along the edge of the rabbit. "This your lunch?"

"Ha. Ha. Ha." Kenyon laughed in a sardonic way. "Why? Do you want a bite?"

I pointed to the bottom right side of the rabbit. "What happened there? The tail's all worn down."

"So would you if I'd been dragging you for half a mile." She waved a hand at the rabbit. "I promised to bring this for the assembly today. The choir's gonna sing. Or maybe shriek." She was also the resident artist in the school and was always having to do this kind of stuff.

"Why didn't your mom drive you?"

"She went up to the mountains last night." Kenyon's voice rose a little in tone as she started to quote her mother. "'Oh, Kenyon, I know I promised to drive you to school, but it looks like it's going to be such a marvelous morning tomorrow. One must be in the mountain streams gathering secret clays.'" Kenyon dropped her voice back into its normal tone. "It was supposed to be a morning to drive your kid over to school and drop off her rabbit." She shrugged one shoulder like she didn't care.

"Couldn't your dad drive you?"

"Archie?" Kenyon curled her lip scornfully. "Archie doesn't drive."

"Lost his license?" I asked sympathetically.

"Never got one." Kenyon deepened her voice and quoted. "'The mechanical world is all too much with us.'" She rubbed her throat and spoke more normally. "So what this means is he's always calling up his friends to give him lifts to this poetry reading or that one. Even Dory—when she's not busy."

"Well, she does have to make a living." I touched the edge of the rabbit with my finger again.

"I know that, stupid." Kenyon shoved my hand away. "And I know she has to live her own life, not just mine. But don't you think a promise should be kept?"

"I guess so," I said uncomfortably.

"And it'd help a lot if I could like the stuff she sells. But even Dory hates the kind of stuff she has to make." Kenyon hunched her shoulders and stuck out her hands from her sides. "She's got all these gimmicks. Like the frog ashtray." Kenyon stretched her mouth as wide as she could and stuck out her jaw and widened her eyes so that they seemed twice as big. Then she raised her tongue slightly and stuck it out. She pointed to her tongue and said something, but it sounded like she was strangling.

"What?"

Kenyon resumed her normal expression. "I said she puts the tongue up so you can leave the cigarette lying on top of it. Or you knock the ash into the back of the frog."

"Oh." I wasn't sure what to say.

Kenyon sniffed. "Well, the tourists from Podunk, Iowa, just love it." She broke into a laugh. "The boutique owners in Monterey make special trips up here to buy her stuff and cart it away by the trunkload."

"You just say whatever comes into your mind, don't you?" I shook my head in wonder. "I wish I could, but it never seems to come out right."

A breeze blew suddenly along the sidewalk and Kenyon had to brace her body against the cardboard rabbit. "You'll learn," she assured me. "It takes practice."

I steadied the rabbit with my right hand. "Do you want some help with that?"

"I can do it." She leaned her head against the top part of the rabbit. Even so, the rabbit twisted between her outstretched hands as if it were trying to break free.

I put my hands up to steady one side of the rabbit.

"By next Easter maybe."

"Yeah, well, the paint runs a little," she warned. The breeze had died down by then, so Kenyon showed me one of her bright purple-and-orange palms. When I looked at the rabbit I could see the parallel tracks where her sweating fingers had made the paint run.

I took my own hands away from the rabbit and inspected the colored smudges on my fingers. "It's washable in water, right?"

"That's what they say." She rubbed her thumb across her fingertips, trying to work some of the paint off.

"It's okay then. Just let me get my stuff." I went back up to our flat and got my binder and my books. I didn't use the schoolbag my parents had gotten me. They thought kids still used them. I brought it to school whenever I had a heavy load of books. Otherwise, though, I left it at home. It gave Sheila and her pack too much to talk about.

When I came out again, Kenyon shrugged the straps of her book bag from her back. "Here, put your stuff in my bag." She held the bag up by its straps so that its mouth was stretched wide open.

I slid my books into the bag. "You want me to carry the bag?"

But Kenyon was already sliding her arms back

through the straps. "I can carry the bag and you. The only reason I'm having trouble with the rabbit is because it's bulky, not because it's heavy." When she had the bag strapped to her back again, she pulled her sleeves free from where they bunched up under the straps. "You ready?"

I was already squatting down to slide one hand under the bottom edge. "Sure."

"Hold on like this." Kenyon slid her palms over the top and bottom edges. "Don't make the mistake of putting your fingers on the painted part like I did."

We started walking. An old dilapidated bus had pulled up at the opposite corner and the men had begun crowding around impatiently, waiting to be chosen for work.

We turned from my street into Pacific Street, which used to be the downtown section. But most of the businesses had moved out of the big, ornate stores there into the new shopping center in the northeastern suburbs, or had left Concepcion altogether. The only things left in the stores besides dust were the fading "For Rent" signs in the windows.

"The City's so outasight," Kenyon said over her shoulder. "You ever miss it much?"

"I miss it a lot." I found myself almost whispering

along the dead, empty street. "I mean the main business here is pumping gas so people can leave for San Francisco or Santa Cruz."

"Well, that's how they advertise Concepcion: two hours to San Francisco, a half hour to Santa Cruz." Kenyon hunched her shoulders and adjusted her grip on her rabbit. "People just sleep here. But they go some-place else to work or have fun. Even the summer people would rather go to the beach at Santa Cruz. They have a boardwalk down there with a roller coaster."

"There's nothing much to do here," I complained. We turned down one of the side streets into the newer section of town; we could move more quickly on the level side-walks. The trees planted near the street were only little things, and the houses all looked the same—like they were mushrooms of concrete and shingles. "I mean, if I had just a little money, I had so many choices up in the City. There was this little theater that used to show triple bills, man, monster films. Westerns. Neat stuff, you know? And if I wanted a snack, I could get a bag of candied ginger or preserved plums or maybe some gwun fun—you know, that's a big fat roll of rice paste with strips of pork and egg and other good things."

"Oh, hey, stop." Kenyon took her hand away from the top edge of the rabbit for a moment and then patted her stomach. "You're making me hungry."

It was funny, but once I'd gotten to talking about Chinatown, it was hard to stop. "I miss almost everything. I even miss Chinese school. I used to go every day after American school. But afterward I could always stop by the comic-book store."

"Outasight." Kenyon twisted her head around to glance at me. "A whole store for comics?"

"Look out." I stopped and held on to the rabbit so Kenyon was pulled up short before she walked into a tree.

Kenyon shifted back onto the sidewalk. She looked at me suddenly. I'd never seen her look so solemn. "It must have been rough coming down here," Kenyon said.

It was the most sympathetic thing I'd ever heard her say about anyone. Even so, I felt cautious. "Kind of."

"I mean, you'd be okay if you just learned to loosen up a little." She stopped at the intersection. School was only a block away now.

"Unh . . . thanks." I wanted to change the subject before Kenyon got started telling me how to improve myself. "Say, how was DUCK SOUP?"

Kenyon took her time answering. "We didn't get to go. Dory has these two friends, Star and Tree . . . a-a-and they came over saying it was a fine, fine night to watch for falling stars. And so Dory and Archie went with them up into the mountains."

"That sounds great," I said enthusiastically.

Kenyon didn't say anything until the light had changed and we had crossed the intersection. Finally she twisted her head around to look at me over her shoulder. "I'll trade your parents for mine then. I think you're lucky to have such a strong family." She turned her head around again.

This close to school there were more kids on the sidewalk, so we moved in closer to the buildings to be out of their way. "I don't know." I chose my words carefully. It was funny having someone to talk to about my parents. "They can be very warm and loving without understanding me at all."

Kenyon slowed down as if she were thinking, then glanced back at me. "It's better than having parents who don't care."

I didn't know how to tell Kenyon about Dad wanting me to be the next Champ of Chinatown, but I thought I'd try. "Sometimes it's like being covered with Saran Wrap, and it's all warm and giving and it doesn't hurt but you can't really ever reach out and touch them. You only think you do through the Saran Wrap. And they don't ever really touch you. They think the

Saran Wrap is enough."

Kenyon managed to shrug her shoulders. "Maybe it would be for most people."

If anyone had told me at the beginning of school that I would be feeling friendly toward Kenyon, I would have said that person was crazy. "You know what? You and me, we're different from the others. I'll get you into Uncle's cove."

Kenyon stopped abruptly. She made such a big thing about dressing like the other girls that I should have known she might be sensitive about being out of the ordinary. "What do you mean I'm 'different'?"

"Come on." I tilted my head back. "You're not going to tell me that you're just like Betsy or Sheila?"

Kenyon lowered her head slightly and stared at me defiantly like a bull getting ready to charge. "I'm not weird or anything."

"I didn't say you were." Nervously I fingered the rabbit's edges. "I mean something may seem weird to people only because they don't know how special that thing really is."

Her head snapped back up. "So I'm weird to just some people?"

"Now wait." I had the rabbit squeezed between my palms so I could lift my fingers and spread them outward in a soothing gesture. "I'm not explaining myself well."

"I understand you just fine." Kenyon adjusted her grip on her rabbit. "We're only a half block away from school. I can take it from here. Thanks a lot."

"I carried it this far, I might as well help carry it the rest of the way." I tried to start forward, but Kenyon wouldn't budge.

"No, it's all right." She emphasized the last two words. "Let go."

I hurried to do what she wanted. The rabbit dropped so hard that its behind got bent. Kenyon set her own side of the rabbit down and then, holding on to it, she shuffled backward until she was standing by its middle.

"Sorry." I squatted down and felt the bottom paws of the rabbit. "The feet got bent a little."

Her foot nudged my hand away. "It's okay. I can straighten them out."

I rose slowly. "I gotta get my books from your bag."

"Oh, yeah, sure." She bent over so that her back was toward me. When I had slipped my books out, she straightened. "Thanks a lot for the help." She started to smooth some of her hair back. It left an orange stain there.

I pointed at her head. "You've got your hair dirty."

"Geezus K. Rist." She started to put her hand back

up to her hair but this time she caught herself. She gave a shrug. "I'll take care of it later. You better hurry. You wouldn't want to be late."

"Yeah, I guess not." I left her as she struggled to lift the rabbit.

II

When school was over, I went home determined to enjoy my parents. If Kenyon envied my family, there must be something there that I wasn't seeing. I promised myself that today I wouldn't get angry at Dad like I had the other day. As soon as I walked into the store, I saw a small cardboard box behind the counter. "What's that?" I set my books down on the countertop and opened one of the flaps to the box and saw it was full of flowers.

Dad seemed embarrassed as he nudged the box with his foot. "I picked some of our flowers."

"Why?" I let go of the flaps and straightened up.

"You'll see," Mom said smugly. She was wiping the dust from a small green bowl with fine wire mesh over its mouth.

I felt the rim of the bowl. "Didn't that use to be in the junkman's window?"

"Not bad for ten cents." Mom held it up for me to admire.

Dad got out his scissors. "Fill the bowl with water, will you?"

I took it into the back room, where the sink was, and filled the bowl. Then, balancing it carefully in my hands, I brought it back to the counter and set it down in front of Dad. By now the store was beginning to smell like a florist's shop.

"Thank you." Dad slipped his fingers through the big loops of the scissors. Then with the scissors he proudly pointed at the flowers in the box. "Those red flowers are peonies. And the blue ones are phlox. The purple ones are early sweet peas." Dad leaned over and took a flower from the box. "And this"—Dad held up a red flower with a yellow center—"is a primrose."

Mom sat down on a stool, and I leaned my back against the counter watching as Dad painstakingly began to cut away the leaves and parts of the stem.

"Your dad makes lovely arrangements of flowers," Mom explained.

Self-consciously, Dad set the primrose into the center of the bowl. "It's nothing really." He took out another primrose, shaking it gently so that several other flowers, which had become entangled with its stem, fell away.

Fascinated, I watched Dad's hands tend the primrose, preparing it for the bowl. I'd always thought of Dad's hands as strong, tough things that lifted hundred-pound sacks of sugar into the air or slapped a basketball hard and fast against the concrete. The hands almost seemed to belong to somebody else: the left hand not holding the primrose but rather cradling it, and the right hand making the scissors dart around the flower—snipping a leaf here and a petal there. The right hand made the scissors almost come alive, so that it seemed more like a sparrow hopping around the flower. I had never known that Dad's hands were capable of such delicate work.

Watching Dad prepare the primrose, I began to wonder about something else that Uncle had said about Dad—I mean, about Dad's drawing pictures. I hadn't believed Uncle at first, because I just couldn't imagine my tough dad trying to make something that looked nice—like a drawing. I would have laughed at Uncle if he had said that Dad also arranged flowers, but I had to believe my own eyes. Dad was actually starting a flower arrangement.

I found myself filled with curiosity. "When did you learn how to arrange flowers, Dad? When you were a kid?"

"No," Dad said quickly, "a lot later—when I was working on the flower farms after your grandfather lost his business. I moved back down here." Dad studied a stalk of sweet peas. There were three flowers on the stem. He intently began to trim the leaves and tendrils away. "Whenever I could get a ride back up to the City, I used to bring some flowers to your momma. That was before we were married."

Mom smiled. "And my mom was always so pleased to see you. You always arranged the flowers so nice."

"In a big old jar of water." Dad frowned. He set the sweet peas as a border to the primrose. Still studying the arrangement, he reached into the box and took a flower. When he finally looked down, he saw he'd taken out another primrose. He snipped a brown-edged petal away from the flower. "But that was hard work on the flower farms. The guy that ran the farm didn't want to use bug sprays, so in the summertime we'd be out there in ninety-five, even hundred-degree weather picking bugs off the flowers." He added the primrose to the center of the bowl.

"You were so brown those summers." She put a hand over her mouth as if she were trying to stop from laughing.

Dad smiled grimly. "Don't ever be a flower farmer, boy."

I looked into the box and picked up a limp stalk with a cluster of small, delicate-looking flowers. "How about these?"

"They'll be fine. Just fine." Dad took them and began carefully cutting the flowers from the stalk so that each of them had as much stem as possible.

"What are those flowers called again?" I asked.

"Wild sweet William." Dad set the flowers along the edge of the bowl. "Also called Phlox divaricata."

"Where'd you learn that?" I asked.

"In one of those library books." Dad shrugged, embarrassed. It was almost as if his knowledge were something to be ashamed of. He added, "But all of that fancy talk"—Dad threw the stalk away and reached for another flower—"won't put groceries on the table."

I was sorry to hear Dad talk like that about his gardening. I could just imagine the small, sensitive boy who tried to make painstaking drawings of flowers; and I could also picture the stern Chinese father who scolded him for wasting paper and pencils. And on that day, the boy had given up more than plants and books and drawings; he had also turned away from a quieter, gentler way of looking at and doing things.

It made me feel sad to think about what had been lost in the past. Only I didn't know how to tell Dad that.

I felt even sadder.

In the long silence that followed, Mom chose her words carefully—like someone who was walking across a floor covered with eggs. "I think," Mom said, "that Uncle is really going to like this present."

"This is for Uncle?" I asked.

"As well as I can remember, his birthday ought to be tomorrow." Dad considered the flowers in the bowl for a moment. "I thought you could bring it down to him after school."

Mom and I watched as Dad worked deftly but surely, readjusting the arrangement.

"I always said you made much better ones than the florists did." Mom swept the clippings into her palm and dumped them into the big empty cardboard box that we used as a trash basket inside the store. Later we would dump the box and its contents into the garbage cans in the back.

"Flower arranging." Dad laughed contemptuously. "What kind of work is that?" He peered into the box and took out a flower. It was white. He frowned and threw it back inside. White was the traditional Chinese color of mourning, and Uncle wouldn't like it.

"Chinese scholars used to like to have flowers around them." Mom picked a bit of damp leaf from her palm.

"I'm no scholar." Dad snipped almost viciously at the next flower he'd taken out of the box. "I never got past high school. Not even a basketball player anymore. Just an old, old has-been."

"Who says that?" Mom brushed some more of the clippings into her palm and threw them away.

"People don't have to say it—I know." Dad thrust the flower into the bowl.

I watched as he added the flowers one by one to the bowl. I was surprised at how restful it was to look at it—soft purples and blues with some red fixed into its heart: like a morning sky rising from the bowl.

And it was pleasing: different shapes and colors all blending almost into a whole, like they weren't flowers any longer—any more than gems are just rocks once a jeweler cuts and polishes and then puts them into a gold setting. I wanted to tell Dad how impressed I was, but all I could think of saying was "The bowl looks great, Dad."

"It's all right." Dad dismissed the bowl with a wave of his hand. It was almost as if he was ashamed of letting me see him arrange the flowers. "It's nothing special to look at."

"No, it's very artistic," I insisted.

"Me, an artist?" A corner of Dad's mouth curled up scornfully.

I rested my elbows on the countertop and leaned

back against it. "Uncle said you used to draw pictures."

Dad wouldn't look at me. He thrust a primrose into the mesh next to the others. Then he reached down and took out another. "I used to do a lot of stupid stuff when I was small. I used to drool when I was a baby." He grinned uneasily at me. "But I grew out of it." It was obvious that he was uncomfortable with our conversation and wanted it to end.

"Do you have any of them? I'd kinda like to see them," I said hopefully.

Dad shook his head slowly, as if it were of stone and very heavy. "Are you kidding? I threw them away a long time ago."

"That's too bad." I couldn't hide my disappointment.

Dad turned to look at me. He seemed puzzled by my reaction. "Why? Those pictures weren't anything but scribbles."

"I still would've liked to see them." I knew that Dad's drawings probably wouldn't have been great art. After all, Dad had only been a kid who had been drawing pictures so he could learn about plants. In fact, I was kind of hoping that his drawings hadn't been too good, so they wouldn't be any better than the ones I did in school. In that way, we would have something in common. Being clumsy like I was, I could feel closer to a dad who drew average pictures than to one who had won all kinds of trophies and got his photo in the newspaper. Being average would have made Dad seem more . . . well, human. "You sure you haven't got any tucked away someplace?"

Dad made a slashing motion in the air with his scissors. "If you can't be the best at something, then you're just wasting your time. You should always drop it."

I wondered if he was going to feel that way someday about training a clumsy son. I felt all broken up inside, and all the little pieces were dissolving.

Dad frowned. "Why are you staring at me like that?" He sounded annoyed again.

"Oh, nothing," I said, trying to sound more cheerful than I felt.

"Umph," Dad grunted skeptically. "You know, you've been acting kind of funny lately. Asking all those stupid questions. And I think it's Uncle who's put all those dumb ideas into your head."

"Uncle's my friend," I said defensively.

"You need friends your own age."

"What's Kenyon then?"

"Well, sure," Dad said desperately, "but you ought to make friends with some guys your own age." He held out one hand. "You see, Craig, you gotta go to the playground and you gotta show those kids that you're just as

good as them." He gave a little nervous, apologetic
smile. "That's what I think, anyway."

I guess Dad had only one way of reaching out to
people. Because it had worked for him when he was a
kid, he thought it ought to work for me.

Mom was still trying to act like a peacemaker.
"Craig, why don't you invite Stanley over sometime?"

I made a face like I'd eaten some sand. "He wouldn't
come."

Dad jerked his head at me. "Why not, boy?"

"He and I, well . . ." My fingers trailed across the
countertop. "We just don't get along so good."

"You see?" Dad nodded his head as if the worst of
his fears had become true. "You're using Uncle's place
to hide in."

I wished I could tell him about my being Preggy
Craigie to the other kids, or the Buddha Man; but I was
just too ashamed. I mean, how could the son of the
Champ of Chinatown be so fat and clumsy? I was afraid
to talk to Dad about all that, because I was afraid he
wouldn't believe me. To have Dad dismiss all the loneli-
ness and misery of the last few months would have been
too much.

I raised my eyebrows and tried to rub the wrinkles
from my forehead. "It's hard, Dad."

151

Dad wiped his hands on a small old dish towel. "I know it's hard, boy," he said almost gently, "but no son of mine would quit."

I looked at the bowl of flowers and thought again of how Dad had given up so many of his dreams when his father had told him to. I had to give him the same kind of obedience. If I wanted to be close to Dad, I had to do it on his terms: I had to become what he wanted me to be. "I'll try, Dad. I'll really try."

I'd never seen Dad look happier. "Good." Dad nodded his head. "Let's go shoot some baskets. And I can show you a couple of head fakes. You'll surprise the kids then when you play them. You know: really impress them."

I stowed my books away under the counter. "Yeah, okay, Dad."

I wasn't having any more luck reaching Dad than I had with Kenyon. The tide pools look so close to one another that maybe to someone else it might look very easy to cross from one pool to another; but to one of the animals in one of those pools it may be a very difficult thing. If you were like that sea slug Uncle had shown me, it could be a trip that would last a lifetime. Only I suppose I had to keep on trying—on their terms if not on mine.

CHAPTER | VII

I

The gate was locked when I went to Uncle's cove the next day after school, but I could see Uncle sitting on his porch, bent over as he worked intently at something. I gripped the wire mesh with my free hand and yelled down to Uncle. "Hey, Uncle. Can I come down?"

Uncle looked up in surprise.

"It's me, Craig. I got something for you." I held up the box into which we had put the bowl of flowers.

Even then, Uncle remained sitting. He put a hand up over his eyes to shade them and stared up at the gate as if he could not really believe I was there.

"It's your birthday present," I shouted.

Uncle set something down and rose slowly from the steps, brushing off his lap and legs. Then slowly he

153

shuffled up the path to the gate. When he was ten feet from me, he asked, "A present? For me?"

"It's from my whole family."

"So Calvin remembered. Maybe he tells everyone I'm one old man." Uncle tried not to seem pleased as he fished his key out of his pocket. He fumbled at the padlock and I set down the box.

"Here, let me." I put my fingers near the mesh. Uncle handed me the keys through one of the holes between the wires, and I undid the padlock and unwound the chain. Then, while Uncle was swinging the gate open, I picked the box up again.

When we reached the porch, Uncle picked up his penknife from where he had first set it down. He folded the blade shut. On the porch rested a little figure no more than two inches high. All around the figure and the porch were long, fine curls of wood.

"What are you doing?" I leaned forward to look at the carving.

"I'm carving *the Dragon Mother.*" Uncle held up the crude figure for my inspection. Then he cleared his throat and spit over the railing down at the cove. "It's too cold out here. You come in and have some good hot tea." Uncle opened his door and waved me inside.

Once I was inside the doorway, I stood there

awkwardly with the box in my hands. "Where should I put this?"

"Anyplace." Uncle closed the door. That was a tall order, seeing how crowded his place was.

For the first time I looked around Uncle's house. I saw the old brass bed in one corner by the window. Most of the rest of the house was filled with huge piles of stuff under tarps and canvases, looking for all the world like ghosts. There was an old-fashioned iron stove in one corner with a box of driftwood beside it—I supposed Uncle had dried the pieces out first. Above the box, several shelves had been built against the wall. They were filled with jars and bottles. Over the bed was an old, faded Chinese calendar that dated back to 1948. In the center of the room, surrounded by piles of old Chinese newspapers and magazines, was a table and several heavy chairs.

While I was busy checking out Uncle's house, he got a fire going in his stove. He chunked a big piece of firewood into it so that it was soon hot in the shack. "You still standing?" he asked. He cleared some newspapers from a chair and added them to a pile right beside it. The pile of newspapers swayed dangerously, but Uncle ignored it. He set the chair down next to me with an authoritative bang and motioned for me to sit down.

I sat down with the box on my lap. Uncle picked up a porcelain washbasin from the cluttered table. "See my spacious bathtub?"

"How do you bathe in that?" With a fingernail I tapped the side of the basin. It rang musically.

"With a sponge." Uncle pantomimed scrubbing himself.

I turned around to look. "Where do you get the water from?"

"My one big luxury. The water main from the Concepcion reservoir goes by here. So I got a pipe up to it. If I want hot water, I heat it up myself." He went over to the window and pulled the curtains back so that the late-afternoon sun could come in. Then he set the basin down beneath the window.

I put the box on the table and waited while Uncle put water in a kettle and set it on top of the stove to boil. Then he dragged a chair over next to me and sat down. Carefully he unwrapped the brown paper from around the box, and just as carefully raised the flaps of the box. "Now look at that." Uncle slowly smiled and lifted the bowl out of the box as if it were something very precious and fragile. He held the bowl at about eye level and turned it around in his hands so he could admire it from all sides. "Just look at that."

I pointed at the flowers. "My dad did all that, and the flowers are from his own garden too."

"Well"—Uncle smiled—"I'm very glad he has his garden now."

Uncle held the bowl while I took the box off the table—the only trouble was that I didn't know where to put it now except on my lap. Uncle set the bowl down on the table and took the box from me, tossing it on top of the washbasin. Then he took the carving from his pocket and placed it near the center. "Just what I need for her."

Right then the water began bubbling out of the kettle, to fall hissing on top of the stove. Uncle jumped from his chair and took the kettle off. He poured the water into a teapot and added two dashes of tea leaves to it. Then he shut the lid on the pot and sat down again. "There's much wonder in the world. It's just like the sea. We only see the tip of it. You know, the highest part. But the sea, it goes down deep, deep. Maybe you go down there, you see the tops of mountains and black canyons. And there are big things in the sea, whales and giant squids. All kinds of animals. But we can't see none of that. Because most of the time we cannot see more than the top."

Uncle poured tea into two cups and set one before me. I picked up my cup and blew on it to cool it off.

"How do you know all that?"

Uncle tried to explain it in Chinese, but I didn't know the words he was using. Finally he had to resort to American. "I got a good . . . you know, a good imagination. I can pretend I'm just like the ones who go before me." With his fingers he pantomimed someone falling feetfirst into the water. "The people under the sea. The holy people. Saints. They swim beneath the water." He wriggled two fingers rapidly, as if someone were swimming.

Listening to Uncle sometimes was like looking through a window into another world. I mean, outside the dirty windowpanes of Uncle's shack, I could see the familiar grayish-black outlines of the cliff face and the green-gray sea flecked with white, and yet it was like I was looking at them now not as part of the American coast, but as the top part of a gate that let you into a magical world. I found myself wishing Kenyon was there.

"Uncle." I tried to sound as hopeful as I could. "May I bring a friend to go swimming?"

He sipped at his tea. *"Of the people of the T'ang?"* he asked cheerfully in Chinese.

I turned my cup slowly around and around on the tabletop. *"A Western person."*

Uncle choked on his mouthful of tea and bent over coughing. When he finally straightened up, the relaxed look was gone from his face and replaced by a bitter, silent expression. "I won't have a *demon* in my cove." He coughed again.

"I'm like them, Uncle, and you let me in here." I tried to pat him on the back to help him with his cough, and instead I wound up spilling my tea on the floor.

Uncle shoved my hand away. "That's different." For emphasis, Uncle touched his chest first and then pointed his fingers at me. "You and me, we're almost related. Your grandfather, he's from the same district in China as me. You go back many, many years, you see we're all related to the First One. It's in the books of the clans." He got up to get some old newspapers from the pile.

In the meantime, I'd already taken some Kleenex from my pocket to dab up the tea. "She's not like the other *Western people*, Uncle."

Uncle stopped reaching for the newspaper. His voice rose incredulously. "You mean your friend is a girl?"

The Kleenex had turned into a soggy lump on the floor. I tried to hold it together. "What's wrong with that?" I got to my feet.

"If you don't know, how can I explain?" Uncle turned to face the windowpanes rattling before a sudden breeze. "How does she know about my cove? You tell her, hunh?"

"No," I said quickly. I slipped around Uncle and began easing a newspaper from the pile myself. "I think she's seen us, but she knows how to keep her mouth shut."

Uncle sat down heavily in his chair and spoke with elaborate care in Chinese as if he did not trust his American. *"American-born, no brains. Like should stay with like. You cannot trust her, because demons will always betray you."*

"That's just crazy talk," I insisted. I picked up the soggy Kleenex and laid the newspaper on the floor and pressed it on the wet spot.

"We helped the demons build this state." Uncle planted his feet firmly on the floor.

"Yeah, I know all about the railroads." With the soggy Kleenex in the center, I began folding the wet paper into a square.

Uncle touched my shoulder so I would look up at him. *"Hear me, boy. We Chinese did more, much more, for the demons. We built the levees that hold back the rivers in the spring, and we drained the marshes so the demons could farm lots of land. We worked their farms and their orchards and their factories. And you know how the demons repaid us?"* He arched one eyebrow.

Still on my knees on the floor, I found myself staring at Uncle as if I were hypnotized. "No, how?"

Uncle took out his knife and pulled open the blade. Then he plucked the carving from the bowl and began whittling angrily. *"As soon as there were enough poor demons to do the work, they all got together and they kicked and beat and chased us from their factories and their farms and their orchards. And the ones they couldn't scare, they killed."* The pile of fine curls of wood grew on his lap. *"They drove us into all the little towns of the T'ang people. It was worth your life just to go onto* Pacific Street. *And even in the towns they would not leave us alone."*

I finished folding up the newspaper and put it outside on the porch so I could take it back to the store to throw away. "But," I said to Uncle, "there are some *T'ang people* that still pick fruit and stuff."

"But only a very, very few, boy. Not like the old days." Uncle examined the carving between his fingers. *"We T'ang people, we had fishing camps up and down the coast and in the bays. We caught fish and shrimp and abalone. There were even some men who knew how to build junks."* With a deep, strong cut at the carving, Uncle deposited a large curl on his lap. *"But the demon fishermen, they got jealous. They got laws passed so we couldn't use junks. And they kept getting more and more laws passed so almost all the T'ang people gave up."* Uncle shaved another large curl from the carving.

"But my father," Uncle continued, *"he wouldn't go. And there were a few stubborn families like ours. Only the place where*

161

we used to work, well, the land there was becoming valuable. The demons tried several times to force us off so they could build what they wanted there." Uncle paused and slowly rubbed the carving between his fingers. The wood now shone like bleached bone. *"Finally some of the demons set a fire, and the demon firemen, they said they couldn't get enough water into their hoses. And a wind came, a great big demon wind, and it blew the fire even hotter."*

With the point of his knife, Uncle began delicately hollowing eyes into the head of the carving. *"Several T'ang people were killed. And when the fire was through, other demons came to steal what little was left."* Uncle was silent while he inspected the carving for a moment. He did not resume talking until he began to work at the eyes again. *"My father tried to get the others to stay and rebuild, but most of them wouldn't. So he and a few friends came here."*

He lifted up the carving in his hand and blew the chips from the hollows of the eyes. *"We tried to still fish for abalone. But the demons, they made it harder and harder for us. Finally the others wanted to quit. My father, he argued. He begged. But his friends left. They said they could make money at other things, things that were safer and less trouble."*

Uncle brushed the shavings from his lap and laughed softly. *"The demons, they said we still took too many abalone. Too many young ones. Too many of the big ones."* He jabbed his knife toward the cove outside his window. *"They said the same thing about the otters, you know that? So the demons drove us from the sea and they killed the otters. Now there are very, very few T'ang fishermen or otters. And there still isn't enough abalone for the demons."* He smiled ironically at me. *"It's a good joke on everyone, isn't it?"* But Uncle didn't wait for my answer. He looked back down at his carving and began to work at its mouth. *"But my father wouldn't leave. He said that if just one of us remembered what had happened, then we would have won a little."* Uncle set the carving back in the bowl and studied it for a moment. Then he turned to face me.

One hand played with the raggedy edge of the jacket he had hung over the back of his chair. *"That's how I got my name. Because I keep my coats so long the tails get ragged. Like the quail. But quails, they may be poor and ragged, but they're one tough bird. They live on when all the pretty pheasants and nightingales have been killed. Somehow the quails go on living."*

"And remembering?" I asked gently in American.

"Yes." Uncle lifted his head defiantly. "The *demons* can take away my big boat. They can take away my catch. But they can't take the sea away from me. That's why I stay. I stay to show the sea belongs to everybody. I stay even if only I know that. So you go ahead now. You laugh at this crazy old man."

"I don't think you're crazy at all, Uncle," I said. There was something about Uncle's quiet, determined courage that made me feel steady inside. I mean, Uncle's stubbornness could be a real pain sometimes, but now I could see that his stubbornness also made him almost a hero—a true hero who didn't need a lot of praise in the newspapers to make him keep on going, or even the approval of others. He was like some big stubborn boulder that had fallen into the sea. There might not be much to see from above, but he was really a giant in his own way. The waves could beat and beat against him but they could only wear away at him, never break him.

For a long while, I didn't know what else to say to Uncle. He made me feel angry and afraid and just all mixed up inside.

As I sat there in his house, I could hear the sea as it crashed against the reef; and as I listened, the sea sounded more and more like a chorus of voices shouting, drowning one another out so that the words could not be understood, only the cries. Cries that faded away into faint whispers that died and were lifted up by the wind. And the cries were of rage and of frustration and of fear.

Finally, though, I managed to shake off some of that mood. I faced Uncle. "I wish I had your courage."

Uncle seemed pleased that I hadn't made fun of

him. Even so, he shrugged. "I don't know. Maybe I'm just too old to change."

"You don't have to change," I said quickly. "Just give in a little."

Uncle studied me as carefully as he might have done with the strands of a net. I felt like he was picking out the weak fibers from the strong ones that were woven together to make me what I was. "Oh-kay. Suppose the *demon friend* comes into the cove. Suppose she gets hurt. What will your poor old uncle do then?"

"You mean like a broken arm or something? She wouldn't tell where it happened. She wouldn't want to get you in trouble."

"*Demons* always make trouble," Uncle said with firm conviction. He put his knife down.

"Uncle, she's not the same as the people who drove you into here. Most of those people are probably dead now."

Uncle began smoothing out the brown paper that his present had been wrapped in. *"Maybe they are ghosts. But I still can hear them."*

Of all the people I knew, Uncle had the best reasons for staying away from others after all the bad things that had happened; but it was also a funny thing that Uncle was also the last person who should be doing that. I

165

mean, Uncle had talked to me about being open to the world. But it seemed that he preferred applying his words to animals and to things, and not to people.

I hunted around for a better way of saying that, though. "You're the one who told me to look at things. Really look at them, I mean. Well, there can be more to my friend just as there can be to the sea and your garden." I chewed on my lip, waiting for Uncle to explode.

But Uncle looked surprised. I don't think he had ever had anyone contradict him during all those years. Uncle added the brown paper to the pile of newspapers, steadying the swaying stack with one hand. Suddenly he gave a laugh. "Well, that teach this old man to talk so much." He grinned. "Oh-kay. You bring the *demon friend* this Saturday. Then I see."

II

When I spoke to Kenyon at school the next day, she was cautious about accepting. This time, though, I was careful not to say anything about how we were different from the others. I just said it would be fun to have some company along and she might like to meet Uncle. She finally agreed, pretending it was a favor to me.

That next Saturday it began to drizzle, but then it let up after a little bit. I finished my other deliveries, leaving Uncle's for the last. After I had loaded up my wagon, I headed for Kenyon's house first since we could then cut down the path to the Coast Road and go straight to Uncle's cove. I'd made a delivery or two to Kenyon's, so I knew the way to her house.

I walked up the slanting streets into the foothills of the mountains. A narrow asphalt road wound its way among the redwoods. The road was kept cleared only on one side and it had no pavement. Drops of water gathered on the branches of the trees and fell with loud splats on the plastic tarp I had tied over the wagon to protect Uncle's groceries.

I began to like my walk among the trees after the rain. The trunks seemed almost a deep burnt red and their needles were a shining green—as if someone had taken a giant emerald and sliced it splinter thin. The ferns, which came up almost to my knee, were a darker, quieter green, so that they seemed to glow. The ferns were almost like the feathers of some giant parrot. Even the dirt looked a rich black color. I'd walked this way before but never noticed how good things looked. The world was there, as Uncle said, if I would just learn to open my eyes.

Kenyon and her mom lived in one of those A-frame houses that looked like the ski cabins I'd seen in a magazine. There was a small, overgrown lawn in front that seemed half daisies and half crabgrass. Kenyon was sitting on the top of the steps leading to her house with a giant bag of shells by her foot on the next step. From that bag she took six shells and put them into a smaller plastic bag, which she then stapled shut.

I put my foot behind the wheel of the wagon to keep it from rolling back. "Why're you out here?"

"Dory and I had this fight." Kenyon put the plastic bag inside another box. "See, I wouldn't go with her last night down to Santa Cruz to help the students protest against the Invasion."

The Americans and the Vietnamese had gone into Cambodia that week. "There were shootings at Kent State. It sounds dangerous."

"What a candyass you are." Kenyon took out some more shells. "At least when I keep out of something, I've got a reason. It won't ever be because I'm afraid."

I thought it would be better to change the subject. "Why are you putting the shells into bags?"

"Bait for sucker fish." She slipped the shells into a plastic bag and folded the top.

"Sucker fish?"

"They always come here to the beach in swarms every summer to breed and raise their young." She tried to staple the bag shut, but her stapler was empty. She made an exasperated sound in the back of her throat. "But they leave each September—thank goodness."

"What do these fish look like?"

Kenyon's voice became prissier and her mouth smaller as she mimicked Mr. Loeb during the science lesson. "'They're notable for their pale skins and for their clustering around transistor radios. What they do during the rest of the year is one of nature's great mysteries. Perhaps when you grow up, one of you boys and girls will be the lucky one to discover what that is.'" Kenyon reloaded the little red stapler. In her own voice, she announced, "They're also called 'tourists' in the vulgar tongue."

"They buy this stuff?" I pointed at the bag in her hand.

"There's one of them born every minute, so the odds are with me." She stapled the bag shut. "I always sell shells during the summer to get some extra money for trashy stuff my folks won't buy for me."

"Like what?" I held the box flap open so she could deposit the bag inside.

"Like TRUE CONFESSIONS. HOLLYWOOD ROMANCES." Kenyon grinned wickedly. "A POLICE GAZETTE can make Archie sulk in his study for a whole day when I visit him."

"Do you like reading that stuff?" Puzzled, I looked at her.

She shrugged her shoulders. "It gives my folks something to talk about when they exchange me."

"You just want me to feel sorry for you." I waved a hand at her.

"So who asked you to believe me?"

I watched her fill a few more bags before I picked up one of them. The shells clinked together as I examined the bag. "These shells aren't like the ones on the beach here."

"The tourists can't tell the difference."

I put the bag back into the big cardboard box where Kenyon had stored the other bags. On one side of the box Kenyon had painted the words: "SHELLS—25¢ a bag." "Where do the shells come from?" I asked Kenyon.

"I don't know." Kenyon put her stapler inside the big cardboard box. "I just go up to this shell store in the City and buy these big bags."

I looked at the price tag still left on one of them. She bought each bag for a dollar, but she probably got ten of her small bags from just one big bag. "There must be some law against what you're doing."

"Didn't you get anything out of social studies?" she asked. "America is based on the principle of free enterprise, better known as 'Give people what they want.'"

"I think we ought to be going."

"Sure, just give me a few minutes." Kenyon opened her front door and put her things inside. "I'll be right back."

I sat down on the steps and waited. It took Kenyon about fifteen minutes to get ready. When she came out of her house, she had a small brown rock. "Here." She thrust it at me.

I took it and turned it over in my hands. It was about two inches long and on one side was the impression of a clam shell, or rather about half of a clam shell. "What's this?"

"It's a fossil clam. I found it by some cliffs up beyond Davenport." Kenyon nodded her head to the north. "It's thousands and thousands of years old. I think it's outasight."

"Yeah." I looked down at it. It was kind of funny to think of a clam being that old—and yet it was special too. Holding the fossil in my hands, I could almost imagine myself on some beach in another time—like the picture in our science textbook. There'd be funny-looking trees in the background and maybe a flying pterodactyl in the sky with a fish in its mouth and dinosaurs moving like huge green clouds among the trees. "Thanks a lot." I stuffed the rock into the pocket of my jacket.

We had no sooner reached the main road when the rain began to fall again, but this time it fell real hard.

Kenyon stared up at the clouds. "Shit."

"Maybe it'll let up." We crouched underneath one of the redwoods for a few minutes.

"I don't think it will." Kenyon's hair clung damply around her head. She pulled up the collar of her old army surplus coat. "I guess this screws up our swim in the cove."

I'd started out by wanting to get an abalone shell to show to other people, but I realized now that it would be fun to visit Uncle just to talk to him. I liked Uncle, even though he could be kind of cranky. "I'm going to go down anyway," I said.

"Most people," Kenyon observed, "know when to come in out of the rain."

"I don't see what difference it makes. I would've gotten just as wet swimming as I will walking in the rain."

"Gee-zus K. Rist, but you're weird." In her own way, Kenyon could be just as stubborn as Uncle.

"Maybe I am." I shrugged one shoulder. "Maybe it's just that I guess Uncle would like to have someone to talk with him. He gets lonely." But I might as well have talked about life on the moon for all that Kenyon understood.

"Oh." She crossed her arms and made a face. "Are you beginning to turn into a Hallmark card? 'Across the miles so far/With memories fond and dear/I send this card to you/And wish that you were here.'"

She gave a little scornful laugh and clasped her hands behind her back. I started to walk away in the rain and Kenyon shouted after me, "Kisses and bullshit."

I turned around then. I could hardly make her out in the soft blur of the rain. "Having a family isn't just a one-way street, you know. You can't just take all the time. Sometimes you have to give."

It wasn't really a bad rainstorm. I mean, the rain wasn't very cold and the wind wasn't blowing, and I could see the clouds overhead: whites and blacks and grays mixing together as if you could see all the energy swirling around in the sky. And the rain was like a sheet of smoky cellophane rippling in front of my eyes so that the hard, straight outlines of things grew softer, almost as if they were about to blend together. And I could feel everything came from the same source.

The sea itself was a green-gray under the rain, shading off far away into a patch of bright light out on the horizon. The gate was unlocked like it always was on Saturday.

There was smoke coming out of the chimney and

there was a warm cheery light coming from the windows. I wondered how I could ever have been scared of Uncle's place. The rain rattled on the roof and ran in long twisting streams from it all around the porch. "Come in," Uncle said when I knocked at the door. I opened it and saw him put his Chinese newspaper down on his lap and push his wire-rimmed reading glasses up on his forehead. "You came here today? In the rain?"

"The gate was unlocked," I said. I went back out and lifted the entire wagon onto Uncle's porch. Then I unwrapped the tarp and brought the carton inside.

"I unlock the gate because I want my groceries." Uncle craned his neck trying to look over my shoulder toward the porch. "Where's the *demon friend*?"

I shut the door behind me. "My friend stayed home."

Uncle sniffed. "A sunshine swimmer." He took off his glasses and put them into a heavy metal case. "Maybe today we'll see a little like the sea people. You ready for your swim, boy?"

"A swim in the rain?" I looked at the raindrops beading the windowpanes.

"You're not a sunshine swimmer too?" He sat back scornfully.

"My towel's all wet, I think." I'd left it outside of the tarp.

"I guess I can spare one." Uncle pretended to inspect me. "You don't look too dirty."

We took off our clothes in Uncle's house before we went to the beach. We had to take the path more slowly than usual, because the lower part that led from the house down to the cove had practically turned into the bed of a stream. The rain seemed to run off from the cliffs onto the path, adding to what fell naturally.

"Not many animals out today," Uncle said when we reached the beach. The sound of the rain on the sea made it necessary for him to speak more loudly than usual. "They like the salt water the way it is. And the rainwater makes the salt water too weak. The animals go lower maybe."

Uncle waded into the water first, swinging his legs slowly. He turned back to me. "Come on, boy."

Shivering, I followed him into the water. I moved my legs stiffly because of the cold. We swam only a few feet from the beach, to a point in the cove where the sand of the beach wouldn't cloud the water. Then Uncle told me to take a deep breath and submerge, but to keep my eyes open. I closed my eyes anyway and took a deep breath and got some rain in my mouth instead. I spat out the rainwater when I had my head under the sea and opened my eyes just a crack. Uncle was pointing over his head. I looked at the surface of the cove. It was like a sheet of green glass that was being changed every moment, and the raindrops made little circles on the surface that rippled and spread outward as if someone were continually drawing patterns over our heads.

We surfaced for another breath and I flipped up on my back. The rain felt like a dozen little hands patting my face. The dark storm clouds paced slowly overhead. I felt a kind of kinship with all the animals huddling away from the surface. It was as if we were beyond the touch of the land. I almost felt a sense of peace.

"Come on, boy," Uncle called. He was already wading onto the beach. "Time to go in. I don't want you getting cramps from the cold."

Reluctantly I kicked back into the shore. Uncle was standing on the beach, hugging himself and rubbing his arms. It did feel cold once I was out of the water.

I was glad when we got back to Uncle's house. He turned the kerosene lamp higher so there was a warm glow in the shack. Then he got me a towel that smelled a little of camphor. I wrapped myself in it. It just about covered all of me, and it was so old that it felt as smooth as velvet. Uncle got a towel for himself and rubbed his skin briskly. "Hurry up, boy. You're dripping water on my floor." He had already started to put on his pants.

Uncle built a big fire in his stove while I finished drying myself and got into my clothes. He had left the teapot on top of the stove and the tea had become very strong, so when I drank it, it felt not only hot but also almost raw.

"Maybe it'll be raining next Saturday." I poured myself a second cup. "I know my friend would like to see everything."

Uncle opened the door to his stove and chucked in another piece of driftwood. *"You can forget that."* Uncle sounded almost relieved to have an excuse. *"I gave the demon friend her chance."*

I stopped with the cup just before my lips. *"But it was raining. She couldn't have known we'd go swimming anyway."*

"Some things you know deep inside you, or you never will." Uncle slammed the stove door shut. *"I don't have sunshine swimmers in my cove."*

I was so excited that I slipped back into American. "You don't really believe that. It's just a handy reason for not letting her into the cove. Please, Uncle. Let me bring her. People are always breaking promises to her."

"I gave her more of a chance than the demons gave me." Uncle sipped his tea. His expression softened a little. *"It's much better if one kind stays with one kind. And another with another."*

I think trying to get Uncle to let Kenyon into his

cove was harder than getting a barnacle to open at low tide to let my finger go feeling around inside. Well, I guess it is hard to change old habits. I just hoped I could explain that to Kenyon.

CHAPTER | VIII

I

The next Monday I found Kenyon already in the school yard, sitting on one of the benches. Her social studies book was open beside her, and her notebook was on her lap as she busily wrote out her answer to a question. She glanced up. "I got to watching TV and forgot my homework." She wrote so fast her pen almost skipped across the page.

I put my books down on the bench and opened my folder. "You want to use mine? I get most of them right."

Kenyon placed her right hand on the page to keep it flat. Her left hand slowly tapped the pen against her lip. "Ummm, no. The only time I tried to copy some-one's, Mr. Loeb got suspicious. I hardly ever get the answers right." She began working intently. "How was your visit to your uncle?"

"We even went swimming." I closed my folder. "By the way, I think that answer's wrong. They probably want the information on page 135." I pointed at the answer Kenyon had just been writing out.

Kenyon wagged her pen back and forth. "I don't think Mr. Loeb can read my handwriting anyway. His eyes aren't as good as yours." Kenyon began scribbling the answer to the next question so that not even I could read it. "But why'd you go swimming in the rain?"

I wriggled my fingertips and let my arm drop as if my fingertips were raindrops falling. "It's neat when you go under the water and you look up and you see the rain hitting the surface."

"Humph," Kenyon tried to say skeptically, but she couldn't help looking interested. "So you think it's worth looking at?"

I remembered my actual reason for talking to her. "Well, actually it wasn't so neat. Or I mean, it'd be just as neat someplace else."

"I don't know." Kenyon wrote the number of the next question with a firm, bold stroke. "Maybe I'll go swimming with you guys next Saturday whether it's raining or not. You got me curious now."

I straddled the bench like it was a horse. "Kenyon, I

told you that my uncle's kinda funny."

"So?" Kenyon glanced up at me suspiciously.

"See, he doesn't really like too many visitors anyway. It was hard enough getting him to invite you."

Kenyon's pen paused over her paper. "What of it?"

"He expected you to come Saturday, even if it was raining."

Kenyon shrugged. "All right, all right. You made your point. I'll go with you this Saturday rain or shine."

I took a deep breath and let the words out in a rush. "He didn't extend an invitation for this Saturday."

Kenyon stopped writing. "What do you mean by that?" she asked sharply.

"I'm sorry, but you can't go with me." I spread out my hands helplessly. "I'll keep working on Uncle though, until he agrees to invite you again. I know how disappointed—"

"I'm not disappointed." Kenyon began working furiously at her homework. "I don't need any favors from you or anybody so just forget it." She pressed her lips together tightly and I could see a little muscle on her cheek twitch like she was clenching her teeth. She also reminded me of one of Uncle's barnacles. When the sea left it exposed on the rock, it had to close up before it could get hurt.

"I know sometimes people let you down—" I began.

"You didn't let me down." Kenyon stabbed the paper with her pen to make a period. "I don't expect anything from anyone and they shouldn't expect anything from me."

I wanted to show her that I was still her friend. "Unh . . . that answer's wrong." I started to open my folder again. "You sure you don't want to—"

Kenyon slammed her book shut. "I've done enough of this stuff."

"Why don't you use mine?" I felt like I had to make it up to her for what had happened, but I only seemed to annoy her even more.

Kenyon capped her pen and threw it into her book bag along with her book. "You can take that homework and shove it up your fundamentals."

"You don't have to be so touchy." I closed my folder and picked it up along with my books. "I'll keep on working on Uncle until I get him to invite you again."

Kenyon shut her notebook. She'd drawn stars all over the cover with her pen. "Forget it. I've got to keep my time free. Dory's gonna take me up to the City to visit an aunt and then we'll really see the town."

"That sounds like fun." I tried to sound cheerful.

"Even if Dory changes her mind, it's no big deal."

Kenyon grasped the straps of her book bag. "And I mean so what if your uncle changes his mind again? He'd probably decide at the last minute that I couldn't visit him." She hefted her book bag up to her shoulder. "That's the way things go, you know? It doesn't make any difference to me one way or another."

"I'm glad that you're not mad." Relieved, I swung my leg over the top of the bench and stood up. "And maybe it works out better this way. Can you keep a secret?"

"Sure." Kenyon shrugged.

I lowered my voice. "Uncle's going to take me diving for abalone once he's trained me."

"Oh, yeah?" Kenyon asked slyly.

"Yeah, it's neat," I went on enthusiastically. "Once he thinks I'm ready, he'll take me down and I'll catch some abalone. I'll bring the shells to school so you can see them. They're real pretty."

"I've seen them already." Kenyon sniffed—like it was no big deal.

"Maybe you've seen some abalone shells," I boasted, "but not like the ones in Uncle's cove."

Kenyon jumped to her feet. "You're so smug. You think you've got so much going for you, don't you?"

"I don't know what you mean," I said, bewildered.

Kenyon glared at me. "You fat candyass. That

Uncle's just making a big fool out of you. All that big talk about training you to dive, that's all a crock of shit."

"He's not fooling me."

"Oh, no? Well, it's no big thing to go diving for abalone. I got a cousin who does it all the time. When the tide is low enough he goes down about ten or twelve feet and he pries the abalone off the rocks. You gotta be able to hold your breath and watch your fingers because when that abalone clamps down on a rock, it clamps down hard; but I don't know how much training that ought to take—even if you're a bad swimmer." Kenyon gave a jerk to the strap of her book bag as the buzzer began sounding a warning to get into the classroom.

I stepped in front of her to block her way. "You're lying."

Kenyon placed her left foot in front of her and then leaned back, putting her weight on her right leg. She smiled insolently. "That's the difference between you and me. I don't care what anybody thinks or does. Nobody can make a fool out of me. Not like some people I know."

"You've gotta be lying," I said. "Uncle's not fooling me."

With the same insolent smile, Kenyon raised the

middle finger of her left hand. "Rotate, Craigles." Then she pushed on past me.

II

I went to the cove right after school. Uncle came out of his house after I shouted and rattled his gate for about five minutes.

"You? Why are you here?" he asked impatiently when he finally reached the gate. "It's not my birthday today."

"I came to find out something." I rattled the gate again. "Do people go hunting for abalone all the time even now?"

Uncle looked at me sharply. "You didn't keep the lessons secret."

"Well, so what?" I gripped the mesh of the gate. "Now I want to know the truth."

"I don't know," Uncle said cautiously. He hunted in his pocket for the key. One hand touched the gate.

"*Western people* do it all the time." I let go of the mesh and backed away. "And they don't make a big thing out of it either. No lessons or other stuff."

Uncle wouldn't look at me. He concentrated instead on the lock. The fingers of one hand reached through the holes of the mesh to hold the lock steady while he put the key in. "They don't do it right." But he wouldn't look at me.

I felt sicker than I ever had during some basketball game. I had trusted Uncle and he had tricked me. Uncle was worse than Stanley or Jim or any of the other kids. At least I knew what they thought of me. I couldn't be any more of a fool to them than I already was. But I had thought it was different with Uncle.

And supposing we had finally gone diving for abalone, I hated to think of what Dad or the kids might have said when I showed them the abalone shells. I'd thought they were so great-looking that I'd impress everyone, but the others would have just laughed at me for making such a big deal out of them. I would have looked like an even bigger fool.

I felt betrayed—first because Uncle had lied to me about how hard it was to dive for abalone. And even worse because Uncle had let me build all these dreams about what would happen when I finally did get some abalone. I could maybe forgive someone for lying to me, but I couldn't forgive him for letting me build all these false dreams about something.

"It doesn't take that much training to go down for abalone. Why did you lie to me?"

It was the wrong thing to say to Uncle. He clenched

the key in his fist. *"So you think I lied to you, hey? You think you know so much. Just like the white demons. Get away from here."* He made shooing motions with both hands. *"Go on. Get out of here, you little demon."*

I turned on my heel and left Uncle still shouting at me.

Well, it was nice for a few weeks while I thought I had friends.

III

I was still feeling pretty bad the next morning about what Uncle had done to me. I'd finished all my morning chores and I'd made my bed and put it away inside the sofa. So now I sat staring out the window, thinking about how Uncle had made such a big fat fool out of me. Dad came out of the kitchen, ready to open the store.

"What's the matter, boy?" he demanded. Dad himself never sat still. He was always doing something, like listening to a game on the radio or reading the newspaper. He couldn't understand why people might sit by a sunny window and think.

"Nothing," I said, looking away from the window.

He clasped his hands behind his back. "Why haven't you gone to school?"

"It's only eight o'clock, Dad." I pointed to the

wind-up clock on the table.

Dad picked up the clock, glanced at it, and set it down again. "There must be some kids there already. You could get up a game."

I sighed and shoved myself up from the sofa. "Right, Dad." I started past him, but he put his hand on my shoulder.

"Wait a minute." He pursed his lips and looked down at me intently. "There really is something wrong, isn't there, boy?"

"No, sir." I stared at his belt buckle uncomfortably. "At least, not really."

"Tell me, boy," he ordered.

I risked a glance up at Dad. For a moment, I let myself hope that he could understand and help me after all. "It's just that Kenyon wants to go swimming in Uncle's cove and Uncle doesn't want her to."

Dad dropped his hand from my shoulder like my shoulder had suddenly caught on fire. He shook his finger at me sternly. "You leave Uncle alone. He's had enough troubles without your bringing more of them into his cove." I saw less sympathy on Dad's face than if I had told him I'd burned down the school.

"Right, Dad." I picked up my books from the floor by the sofa bed.

Dad planted his fists on his hips. "You show those other guys some of the tricks I taught you."

"Right, Dad." I got my jacket from the closet. It was almost a relief to escape from the flat. I took the steps two at a time and trotted for the first block to school. I didn't want Dad shouting anything to me while I was on the street.

I should have known that Dad wouldn't give me any helpful advice—he only wanted to give me instructions on how to be an all-American boy. But I thought that maybe he might be right. Maybe I ought to try even harder in a game and really make friends with the other guys—especially since I'd managed to lose the friendships of Kenyon and Uncle.

By lunchtime I had worked up enough nerve to try and keep my promise to Dad. I mean, I'd played in lots of games before this, but I was determined to make a real impression this time. I almost lost my courage, though, when I walked onto the basketball court near the street side of the school. All the other guys looked so disgusted when they saw me; but since they needed a tenth player, Jim got stuck with me on his team.

Stanley, who was on the other side, told the rest of his teammates not to bother guarding me.

Bradley, who was on my team, shook his head. "Don't

worry." He grinned. "We'll beat them. Then your cousin will have to eat his words."

I nodded stiffly. I could feel my stomach tightening just like it did before any game. My breath was coming just a little short from all the excitement; and my legs felt a little weak. I told myself that this was just a lunchtime game. It wasn't like it was for a world championship. But I don't know. I guess when you're trying to prove yourself, every game is an important one. If not for my sake, then for Dad's.

When Stanley's team in-bounded the ball, Stanley clapped his hands and called out, "Hey, over here." They passed the ball to Stanley and he pivoted. He had this real funny smile on his face as he dribbled straight toward Bradley and me.

Bradley crouched and spread his arms. He was the tallest kid on the court, so when he spread his arms he covered a lot of ground; but he wasn't quick enough for basketball. One moment Stanley was standing and grinning at Bradley while leisurely dribbling the basketball. Then the next moment he was moving like the wind as he drove inside of Bradley and pulled up short. I flung my arms up like Dad had been telling me for almost a year, but Stanley was already jumping into the air. He arched a high, graceful shot that sent the ball swishing neatly through the net.

"Jeez," Jim muttered to us, "he caught you both flat-footed."

I thought that was bad enough, but at that moment I heard a man shouting. "Get more motion into your arms, boy. They're not made of wood."

I just stood there for a moment, afraid to look.

"That's all right, boy. You'll get the points back." The man had begun to clap; and even though he must have been out in the open air, his clapping sounded thunderous. Finally, I turned around to see Dad standing by the fence. He was maybe fifty feet away, but I could hear every word distinctly in his booming voice. "Remember: more motion." He held his arms above his head and then moved them back down toward his hips.

Our old pickup truck was behind him. There were some cartons in the back. I guess he'd driven over to the wholesaler and picked them up. He must have been driving back to our store when he'd seen us playing so he'd stopped to watch.

"Hi, Stanley." Dad waved to him. Stanley waved back. Then Dad motioned to me. "Now hustle, boy. Hustle."

Dad sounded so hopeful that I knew I couldn't disappoint him. I felt my stomach tightening as I trotted toward Jim. We were only playing half court, so Jim was in-bounding from the mid-court line.

"Go on." Jim nodded his head impatiently toward the basket.

I wheeled around and started to move with all the others. Somehow I wound up by the basket. Harold went over to guard me, but Stanley glanced over his shoulder at us. "I told you, man, don't bother guarding him. Help me double-team Jim." Harold swung over to guard Jim, who was the best shot on our team.

When Jim saw Harold heading for him, he passed the ball to Bradley, who held the ball high over his head. That way nobody could steal it from him, which was what happened whenever he tried to dribble. Jim kept twisting and whirling like a top, trying to break free from Stanley and Harold, but they kept him sand-wiched between them.

"Pass it to Craig," Jim bawled to Bradley.

Bradley saw me. I spread my hands halfheartedly and Bradley threw the basketball to me.

I told myself that I had to do well this time. After all, Dad was watching me. Now you know that when I practice with Dad, I'm not the greatest shot in the world, but I can at least catch the ball before taking a shot. Right now, though, in a game with Dad watching me, I wasn't sure I could even do that much. I don't suppose I would have done any better if Dad hadn't been there, but I could just feel his eyes on me. I told myself that however badly I might play in any game after this, I just had to be good during this one.

In all the sports books that I'd read in the library— the books with titles like COURAGEOUS CENTER or FEROCIOUS FORWARD—there's always one moment at the end when the goat of the team becomes a hero. If there were any justice in the world, there would be one moment in a person's life when he or she hits a home run or catches a touchdown pass or makes a winning bucket; but life doesn't go that way, I guess.

The moment I told myself that I had to play well, I could feel my arms and legs begin to stiffen as if somebody had changed them into wood. I was lucky to move them at all. I put my hands out to catch the ball and panicked when I felt it graze the palms of my hands as it went past. It bounced off my chest, but I clutched it with both arms like I was drowning and it was a life preserver. All right, so maybe I hadn't caught the ball in a pretty enough way to get a bubble-gum card made about me, but at least I had caught it. I felt a brief moment of relief.

"Shoot, boy," Dad called. I could hear the anger creeping into his voice. I pivoted. A grinning Stanley came over to cover me.

Dad had taught me to fake with my head and shoulders so the opposing player would think I was going to drive in. That would keep him planted on the court while I took my shot. I jerked my head and shoulders forward, but I was so busy putting the head fake on Stanley that I didn't pay attention to what he was doing. He reached straight for the ball and slapped it out of my hands while I was busy faking. Stanley got the ball, and before Jim or Bradley or any of the others could get a hand up, Stanley was already leaping into the air to bank the ball off the back-board through the rim.

So much for the head fake that Dad had spent so much time trying to teach me. He said it would impress the kids and it did, but the wrong way. Jim looked totally disgusted with me. "Shit," he said. "He took that ball right from you." Stanley passed the ball to him and he dribbled back toward the mid-court line.

I tried to keep my head up and look at the others. I told myself that I'd just get those points back. Just like Dad was shouting at me.

"It's my fault." Bradley walked over to us. "I passed it too hard. He had to get control of the ball."

"Hey," Jim said, "this isn't some ladies' tea. I want baskets, not excuses." He stepped over the mid-court line and passed the ball to Bradley. Bradley waited until

194

Jim had stepped back onto our half of the court and then tossed the ball back to Jim. Without watching for either of us, Jim began driving down the court.

"Hustle, boy, hustle!" Dad shouted. Bradley glanced in surprise toward Dad.

"It's my dad," I explained. I ran after him. I told myself I'd not only show Dad, I'd show Jim and all the other kids I could play just as well as them.

It was a couple of plays later that I wound up free under the basket again. Jim passed to me this time. He tried to make it soft. I started telling myself that I just had to play well this time. I mean, it was fine to tell myself that I'd get the points back and that I'd show Dad and the kids that I could play all right; but now was the time to put up or shut up.

I could feel myself tensing again until my arms and fingers were stiff. I watched in horrified fascination as the ball slowly arched downward toward me as if in slow motion, growing larger and larger and larger like there was a big orange comet falling toward me. I tried to stop it with my hands, but they were now about as useful for catching a basketball as two Ping-Pong paddles. The basketball slipped easily through my hands and hit me in the face—not real hard, but it hit my nose in just the right spot so that the tears started coming into my eyes.

I tried to wipe away the tears so I could see. I could hear shouting and gasping while the others fought to get the ball.

Then I felt a strong hand on my arm and I was steered, almost propelled, over toward the sidelines. "You okay?" Bradley asked.

"Yeah, sure." Frustrated, I wiped at my eyes with my free hand, blinking my eyelids rapidly so I could see a little. "The ball just hit me the wrong way, you know? I'm not really crying."

"Yeah." Bradley grunted sympathetically. "I saw the ball hit you. My eyes'd be watering too."

"Bradley," I heard Jim shout, "where the hell are you, man?"

"We better get back in the game." I tried to walk back onto the court, but Bradley still had hold of my arm and he held me back. "You just wait, okay?"

"Okay."

"You want me to take you over to your dad?" Bradley asked.

"God, no." I shook my head violently.

"Suit yourself." Bradley gave me a pat on the shoulder and heavily trotted back to the court.

If only I could have made just one good play. Just one. I didn't even have to make a basket. Just knock away a pass or something. Then I could have made Dad proud of me. But instead here I was standing on the sidelines with my eyes watering.

"You all right, boy?" I heard Dad call from behind me. We were still about thirty feet apart.

"It's just my eyes watering." I didn't turn around. "I'm not crying."

"Well, you ought to get back in there," Dad said. "Your team needs you."

My team needed me as much as they needed a dead horse, but I didn't say that. I waited until the tears had stopped and it just felt like someone was pinching my nose. Then I went back onto the court. Dad started his cheerleader act all over again.

"Good." Stanley grinned when he saw me. "Your side was just beginning to catch up."

I don't need to tell you. I mean, you would have already guessed that we lost the game. Except for Bradley, everyone else on my team stopped passing to me, and in some ways I wish Bradley had given up too. But Bradley would glance toward the fence where my father was, and then he would look at me, and my stomach and arms and hands would tighten as I knew Bradley was going to pass to me no matter what Jim or the others screamed to him.

When the buzzer sounded ending noon recess, I

heard Jim muttering to Harold that I was one "sad case."

"His dad's here," Bradley growled to Jim, "so shut up."

Jim just looked at me and shook his head like he felt sorry for my dad. They all walked toward the classrooms, but I stayed on the basketball court, trying to work up enough nerve to turn and face Dad. I wanted to apologize to him for the way I had played; but I wasn't sure that he wanted to be seen talking with me.

Then I heard a truck starting up. I twisted my head around. Dad was already pulling away from the curb in his truck. I remembered what Dad had said about his drawing: If you weren't good at a thing, drop it. Maybe I could tell him I wanted to drop basketball and the other sports. I mean, he knew for himself just how bad I was at basketball. I thought he was leaving without a word to me because he was so embarrassed by my performance.

I should have known better.

"Dad—" I began to say.

Dad stopped the truck for a moment. He leaned across the seat to poke his head out of the window on the right side of the truck. "Good game," Dad said. "You played real hard. Get up a game after school and bring all the guys over to the store afterward." He waved at me cheerily.

I didn't know what to say at that moment. How could

Dad just ignore what he had seen during the game? He ought to know by now how badly I played and how the others acted toward me, but it was as if all the humiliations had been to someone else. Dad saw only what he wanted to see.

IV

I would have loved to talk with Uncle after school or even speak a little to Kenyon, but I didn't have anyone. I could only go back to the store and face Dad.

The moment I entered the store Dad asked, "How come you're back so soon? Wasn't there a game after school?"

"I didn't feel like it, Dad."

Dad shook his head and rubbed the side of his Pepsi bottle nervously with his index finger. "I told you to play with the kids after school and then bring them over. You kinda ruined our surprise." Dad drank the last of the Pepsi from the bottle.

"Craig didn't ruin the surprise," Mom insisted. "He can show it to the other kids tomorrow."

"I was kinda hoping to see their faces, though." Dad put his empty Pepsi bottle down on top of the counter. Then he bent over and reached for something underneath the counter so his voice came up a little muffled.

"We were saving this for your birthday, but . . ." He set a big white paper bag down on the countertop. Mom picked up the empty Pepsi bottle before Dad could knock it over with the bag.

"What is it?" I asked.

"Open the bag and see." Dad shoved it closer to me. I set my books down on the countertop and began to tear the paper bag open. It was a new basketball, sitting in a display carton with a hole in its side that showed the ball. The basketball was colored a bright red, white, and blue, and it was turned so I could see Rick Barry's signature.

Dad smiled at me happily. "Man, oh, man," he said, "when you bring this to school tomorrow, the kids are really going to be impressed."

Maybe I could have controlled myself if I hadn't had all that trouble with Uncle and Kenyon, but I was still hurt and angry that Uncle had made a fool out of me, and I was sure that Kenyon would be so mad at me that she would be cooking up some new humiliating nick-names to stick to me. Dad had just watched me play a rotten game of basketball—a game so rotten that all the other kids except Bradley acted like they were mad at me. And now Dad seemed to think that a new basketball made up for all that. Even worse, he expected me to take it to school to impress the kids—when I knew that all they would do was laugh at me. It made about as much sense to give me a basketball as to give some prisoner a new whip so his torturers could use it on him. I hated the sight of that basketball. I hated the basketball so much that it hurt inside me.

There was a long uncomfortable silence while I just stared at the new basketball. Finally Mom spoke to me. "Well, thank your dad."

I tried to remember my manners, but somehow the words came out of my mouth sarcastically. "Oh, yeah. Thanks."

Dad pressed his lips together like he was a little hurt that I hadn't made more of a fuss about the basketball. "Well, it's something you'll use. How about trying it out?" He tore the flaps from the carton without waiting for my answer.

The last thing I needed now was to have Dad tell me what I had done wrong in the game. "No, Dad, please. Not now," I begged.

He already had the ball in his hands. "You sure?" He sounded hurt, but I'd been through so much in the last few days that I didn't care.

"Yeah." I closed my eyes for a moment. "I'm sure."

He shifted the basketball from one hand to the

other and then back again. "But if you want to take this new basketball to school tomorrow, you better get used to playing with it."

I actually winced—like someone had poured acid into a cut. I looked up at Dad. "I can't take this to school, Dad. The kids'll just laugh at me."

Puzzled, Dad held the ball steady in both hands. He stared down at it. "You want some other player's signature, is that it?"

I guess it was like something had been dying inside me all these months in this crummy little town: something that had been dying and drying up inside me like the flowers that wither on a hillside during the hot summer. And with those words it was as if Dad had just flung a lit match on top of everything so that it burst into flame and I could feel the anger roaring to life inside me.

"Is that the only reason you can think of?" I asked. I almost spat the words out. "You saw me today. I'm small and fat and clumsy and slow."

Dad pretended he was studying the basketball. "You just need a little practice. That's all," he insisted.

"Even with practice. Dad"—I took a breath before I plunged on—"will you face it? I'm just not good at basketball." Mom was shaking her head for me to shut up. But it was like whatever was inside me was burning so hot and so fast that if I didn't let the words out, I'd explode.

"Well," Dad said slowly, "maybe football or baseball can be your game." He finally looked at me. "But you've got to have something so you can go out and show the American kids."

"Why?" I was so mad that I didn't care what I said.

Dad managed to control his own temper. He took a deep breath and let it out in a rush and as patiently as he could, he said, "My father would have slapped me if I had said something like that to him." Dad drummed his fingers on the sides of the basketball. "You be more respectful to me."

"Please. Just tell me why you always want me to do all of that stuff?"

Dad hesitated and then nodded his head firmly. "All right. You want the truth? Well, I'll give it to you. You gotta show these American kids what you can do. You're a Chinese from Chinatown. Not like Stanley or Sheila. What they think of you is gonna be what they think of all the other Chinese. Craig, you got a chance like I never had."

I picked up my books and folder from the countertop and threw them on the ground. They slid against the bin of potatoes. "Will you quit trying to live my life for me? Why can't you let me make an impression the way I want? Why does it have to be sports? I don't want to play sports. I'm not good at sports. I'll never be."

Dad held the basketball between his fingertips, turning the ball slowly. "Not without any practice." He threw it to me and I caught it.

Deliberately I dropped the ball. "Dad, I don't like sports. Any of them. I never want to practice them again."

Dad sat down on a stool. He leaned forward, resting his elbows on his thighs. He clapped his hands together two or three times nervously. "I can understand that. Not much future for a Chinese in sports. I mean, look at me. Couldn't make a living at it no matter how good I was."

"That's not the reason, Dad." I put my hands on top of the counter and leaned toward him urgently.

"It's all right." He waved one hand at me. With his other hand, he massaged his forehead and looked away. "If you're a failure, then you're a failure."

"I don't think—" I began, but Mom shook her head again.

"Just go upstairs, Craig," she said.

I picked up my books and folder from the floor and left.

All in all, I'd say that I had done a pretty good job in just two days. I'd not only broken up with my two friends in Concepcion, but I'd also managed to insult Dad. The only other person I could talk to now was Mom, and I could probably make her mad at me too with just a little effort. Then that would only leave myself to talk to; and I was such an idiot that I wasn't even sure I wanted to talk to myself.

I'd managed to make myself such an all-American louse.

CHAPTER | IX

I

Dad didn't talk to me all that night or the next morning. It was like I was dead. I expected Kenyon to have invented a whole new set of nicknames for me when I got to school, but she ignored me just as Dad had done.

When I got home after school, I didn't go into the store. Instead, I went through the front door and up the steep front stairs to our flat. I didn't want to talk to anyone. I was going to stay up there, but then I had second thoughts because there was always the chance that Mom or Dad would come up to use the bathroom. So I went down the back stairs into our garden.

The zinc tub in the back had dried out, so I turned it over and sat down on top of it. Dad's garden wasn't much compared to the gardens of those tract homes with their large lawns and flower beds, let alone a park. But sitting there in the garden by myself, I felt strange inside.

Before we had moved down here, "springtime" had always just been another word in a spelling book to me; but now I could see and smell what springtime really meant. There were little green buds appearing on the bare branches of the fuchsia plant. It hadn't been dead after all; it had only been asleep until the time had been right. And here and there around the fuchsia plant were patches of green grass blades.

Across the backyard, on the opposite side, were Dad's flower boxes. All of the transplanted flowers were taking to their new homes, and even though Dad had used a lot of the flowers for Uncle's present, there were still quite a few left in the flower boxes, so there were little rectangles of red and blue and purple that almost seemed to glow in the soft, gray light of the backyard.

The day itself was one of those sunny days after the breezes have shoved the smog and dust out of the air so that the sky is so deep and bright a blue that it almost hurts to look at it. But Dad's garden was separate from the glare. In the afternoon, the garden was completely shaded by the surrounding buildings. I felt almost like I was sitting at the bottom of a pool filled with a soft, gray liquid that could ease the hurt and strain in my eyes that came from having to look at things in the glare of the outside. I wished I could tell Dad right then what a good thing the garden was, but I just didn't know how.

The two Lopez kids next door were pounding away at something that belonged to their car. I suppose it was a fender. The old basketball was out there. I picked it up. The letters spelling VOIT had almost worn away, but otherwise it seemed good enough to me. Dad, though, seemed to think that was a good enough reason for getting rid of it. Like he said, if a thing isn't the best, drop it. At first I began bouncing the ball in rhythm to their hammering, but when the ball bounced too high for me to get, I let it roll away under the fuchsia plant.

Somehow I seemed as clumsy with my friends as I was with a basketball. I had made such a big deal in my own mind about how I was beginning to see people and things. Instead, I'd turned Kenyon against me. Well, I could live with that. I'd hurt Dad's feelings, but I could even live with that. What hurt the most was how Uncle had fooled me. After all his talk about how we should look at things specially, he'd lied to me. I felt . . . well, like I'd been betrayed. All in all, I'd done a good job of making almost everyone mad at me and myself mad at almost everyone else.

After the back door of the store had closed, I heard

Mom's light steps in the alleyway. I jumped off the tub and got the basketball and began bouncing it diligently around the backyard. I dribbled carefully to the mouth of the alley and saw Mom slamming the lid down over one of the garbage cans.

She came around the corner. "I thought it was you," she said. She held out her hands. "I feel like some exercise myself. Mind if I shoot some baskets?"

"Be my guest." I tossed her the ball.

Mom had played basketball under the old rules for girls' basketball, where they didn't allow much contact. It had been more passing and accurate shooting. When Mom shot now, the ball went in clean through the rim. She rebounded her own shot.

"I wish I could do that," I told her.

Mom paused. "You use too much force, I think. Try a softer touch. Like this." The ball went through the rim cleanly again.

I rebounded the ball for Mom and bounce-passed it to her. "Is Dad still angry today?"

Mom dribbled the ball. "More or less. You could have been more tactful yesterday." She bounced the ball up high and caught it. "You have to realize that he's very sensitive, even though he tries to act so tough."

I went over and stood underneath the basket to get

ready to rebound Mom's next shot. "Maybe I ought to tell him how sorry I am."

"That would just start the argument all over again," Mom warned. "Let your dad cool down first." Mom sent the basketball arching up high through the air. It sank cleanly through the basketball rim a third time.

I grabbed the ball after one bounce and held it against my hip for a moment while I scratched the tip of my nose. "You think I ought to do that with Uncle and Kenyon? They're both mad at me too."

"Sounds like you've been busy this week." Mom motioned for me to take a shot. "How'd you ever do that?"

I tried to copy what Mom had done but I still used too much force. The ball hit the rim with a loud clunk and then the ball bounced up in the air. I managed to chase it down before it bounced into Dad's flower boxes. I paused for breath. "Well, Uncle made this big deal about how I had to have all this special training to go diving with him, but it was a lie. And Kenyon, well"— I shrugged—"she wanted to go swimming in Uncle's cove but Uncle's changed his mind so she blames me now." I dribbled the ball back over toward Mom and passed it to her.

She bounced the ball between both hands slowly.

"Your uncle and your dad don't tell lies deliberately. They have these expectations and they want things to match their expectations. It's like having a road map for a place you've never been to. Sometimes a town and the streets aren't exactly like the map says they should be. The bad thing is that sometimes people get mad at the town when they ought to get mad at the map." Mom hefted the ball in her hands and took a shot. She made another bucket.

I was going to tell Mom how stupid I thought it was to blame the town instead of the map; but then I realized that I was just as guilty as the others. "I guess that's why I got so mad at Uncle. I didn't expect him to fool me." I looked at Mom helplessly. "What can I do to make them my friends again?"

Mom folded her arms across her stomach. "Don't try to force things. Just leave them alone for a while and wait until you have something you can agree on. Who knows? They might even start changing their road maps."

I didn't feel as sure as Mom did, but it was harder for me to argue with her than with Dad. She didn't try to outshout you or even try to outargue you with a lot of reasons. She gave a matter a lot of thought and then stated the best reason she could and you could go on being wrong if you liked.

I crouched slightly, resting the ball on the palm of my

211

left hand, and then pushed the ball off with my right—but trying to use as light a touch as I could. The ball arched slowly in the air. It almost went in but hit the rim and bounced out.

"Pretty close," Mom said encouragingly.

II

I tried to do like Mom had suggested, even though I didn't think it would do much good. I just didn't see how things could get any better. I was friendly to Kenyon, but she was cold. There weren't any joking insults, only a cool politeness—which was a strange thing to see in Kenyon. Dad would answer me sullenly but he seemed to be waiting to defend himself against some other complaint of mine.

As for Uncle, when I made my deliveries that Saturday, I tried to talk to him; but he only shouted through the door for me to go away because he wanted to take a nap. I asked him if I could go for a swim in his cove. When he didn't say anything, I didn't press the matter but left.

The next week, Dad and Kenyon acted just as they had the other week. I got kind of discouraged then. Mom said it would take time, but I didn't know. They both seemed like the stubborn kind with long memories.

But I remembered what Dad had said in one of our practices: that no son of his would quit. And if I was Mom's son, I ought to have some of her patience. So I went on trying.

At the end of the week, when I visited Uncle again, I found him actually sitting on his porch. He was pointedly staring out at the cove.

"Hi, Uncle." I set the groceries down beside him.

Uncle said nothing but went on looking out at his cove. His lips parted for a moment as if he wanted to say something but didn't quite know what, so I thought I'd help him.

I pointed to the carton. "Would you like me to take these things into the house?"

Uncle turned to face me, but then his nerve failed him. He merely grunted and shook his head. He was still a little mad at me.

The week after that was the hardest of all. It didn't look like I'd ever make friends again with Uncle or Kenyon, or get Dad to act more like himself. Even so, I forced myself to keep trying. If I could work that hard in a game with the kids, I ought to be able to give some of the same energy to making up with my friends—no matter how clumsy I might be.

But that Saturday, things began to turn around finally.

Uncle was out on the porch like the last time, still giving me the silent treatment. But this time when I asked him if he wanted me to take his groceries inside, he managed to shrug his shoulders.

I interpreted that as meaning he didn't care what I did with his groceries, so I picked up the carton and took it inside. When I came out, I wiped the sweat from my forehead. "Well, I'll see you." I tried to sound cheerful.

"Are you hot?" he asked suddenly.

"A little." I pumped my arms in slow circles. "Everyone seems to be stocking up on groceries this week."

Having said a few words to me finally, he found it easier to say a few more. "Go for a swim then." He jerked his head at the cove.

"I'd like to, but"—I motioned to the empty wagon— "I didn't bring a suit or towel."

"Swim in your underwear then." Uncle waved a hand at me. "I can loan you a towel."

"That's really kind of you." I put a foot on the first step. "Will you go swimming too?"

Uncle sighed. He wasn't ready to forget everything that had happened. He leaned his head back against the railing. "No."

I got the towel from inside and went down to the beach. I swam for only a little while because the water was still very cold. Uncle had shifted his position on the porch so he could watch. When I had toweled myself off, I went back up to Uncle's house and hung the towel on a railing to dry. "Well, thanks a lot."

Uncle flicked his hand up and down just once. "It's nothing."

I finished dressing. "Maybe you'll feel like swimming with me next time."

"You mean for abalone?" Uncle asked cynically.

"It doesn't matter," I said carefully. "The swim's enough."

Impulsively I reached my hand into my jacket pocket. I'd been waiting for an opportunity to give my present to Uncle and now seemed like a good time. "Here, Uncle. It's a little late, but this is another birthday gift."

Uncle took it from me and stared down at the small brown rock in his hands. "What is it?"

"It's part of a fossil clam." I turned the rock over so he could see the impressions of the clam shell. "It's really old. Maybe as old as the dinosaurs."

"The what?" Uncle asked.

"Dinosaurs. They were like gigantic lizards." I raised my arms above my head and stomped around a little.

Still skeptical, Uncle weighed the fossil clam in his hand. "Thank you for the funny rock." He ran his fingers over the ridges of the fossil. "It must have taken a long time to carve."

"My friend found it, Uncle." I picked up the box of garbage. "She didn't make it."

"Sure." Uncle still didn't sound convinced.

I couldn't help laughing as I eased the box into the wagon. "You'd like my friend, Uncle. She can be as stubborn as you."

Uncle sat up straight and stuck out his chin. "I'm not stubborn. It's everyone else who's stubborn. They should see the right way to do things."

"Meaning your way?" I grabbed the handle of the wagon.

Uncle wrinkled his nose and then sniffed. His face broke into a grin. "Of course." He hesitated and then held the fossil clam in front of me. "Now you tell truth. You carve this. Or your friend."

I had thought Uncle would be as impressed by the fossil as I had been, but he seemed to think I was playing some elaborate trick on him. "My friend got it around some of the cliffs to the north." I added, "She likes looking for things by the seashore."

Uncle's fingers closed around the fossil. He drew his hand back and rested it on his lap. "This *demon friend* does, hah?"

"I said she was a lot like you, Uncle." I circled the wagon around so I could go up the path.

"So you still see her?" He set the fossil down on the porch beside him.

"Unh, not exactly." I stood there awkwardly for a moment with both my hands gripping the handle of the wagon behind my back.

Uncle tilted his head back a little. "Because she couldn't swim here?"

"Well, you know." I shrugged and studied the path up toward the top.

"But you have other friends now?" Uncle sounded like he was actually worried.

"I'm really too busy to have time for that kind of stuff." I started up the path and gave a jerk to the handle to pull the wagon along. "I gotta be going." I took my right hand temporarily away from the wagon handle to wave a good-bye to Uncle. I was determined to do things Mom's way and not push him.

III

Then late Thursday afternoon, Mom, Dad, and I were all in the store when a familiar figure came shuffling through the door. Dad paused with a lit match in his hand, his mouth opening as he plucked the cigar from between his lips. "Uncle?"

Uncle sized up Dad. "Hello, boy. It's a long time."

"Unh, yeah," Dad said in wonder, "a real long time." He remembered in the last moment to shake out his match before he got burned.

I came from the back of the store silently and stood nearby. At first, though, Uncle would not look at me. Instead he smiled at Mom. "This is your wife?"

"Yeah, Jeanie, this is Uncle *Quail.*" Dad motioned vaguely between Mom and Uncle.

"Pleased to meet you, Uncle." Mom smiled her pleasantest smile. "I've heard so much about you."

Uncle grinned. "Don't hold it against this old man."

Dad came bustling from around the counter. "Can I get you a soda, Uncle? No, you probably want tea. Jeanie, would you—"

"Everything's fine, boy. Just fine." Uncle patted Dad on the arm. "I just go for a walk. Now I rest." Uncle turned his head slightly. Just in front of the rack of potato chips, he saw a roll of butcher paper that was standing on end. He sat down slowly on it. "I heard you have a garden. With flowers."

"It's not much." Dad tried to shrug it off like it was nothing. "Just something to keep Jeanie happy."

Slowly and deliberately Uncle shook his finger at

Dad. "And you too, boy. I'm old but my memory's still pretty good. You used to want one."

Dad waved his cigar in the air. "I wanted to do a lot of things when I was a kid. Okay, so maybe I wanted a garden for two weeks. I probably dropped that idea and wanted a pony instead. You shouldn't make such a big thing out of it, Uncle."

Carefully Uncle planted a hand on either knee. "Maybe you too small to remember good. Maybe I remember better."

I was doing my best not to smile, because it was so much fun watching the two of them argue. Neither Dad nor Uncle was used to giving in to someone. But Uncle was the older of the two and Dad had been raised not to contradict his elders. After they said a few more things back and forth, Dad shrugged. "Have it your way, Uncle," he said tolerantly, as if he were doing his best to humor a cranky old man. He set the cigar in his mouth and clamped his teeth down.

Even in victory, Uncle didn't relax his rigid posture one bit. He nodded his head solemnly. "I would like to see this garden."

Dad took out his cigar. "It's not as fine as your cove."

"Of course," Uncle said matter-of-factly, "but show it to me anyway." Uncle rose from the paper roll and waited for Dad to lead the way.

"It's in back." Almost shyly, Dad led Uncle through the back room and into the garden. I followed them.

Uncle smiled as he shuffled past the fuchsia plant toward the flower boxes. "Pretty. Very pretty."

Dad put his hands on his hips and looked around, satisfied. "They add a little color back here. It needed a little cheering up, you know?"

Uncle turned around slowly, inspecting the rest of the backyard. His eyes fixed themselves upon the basketball hoop. "Good. It's late. But you have the things you wanted when you were small."

Dad rubbed the side of his nose. "Well, now—"

Uncle held up his hand abruptly. "No, it's true. I think your father want you to be too much like him; but you should be like you, yourself."

"My father did his best, though," Dad said uncomfortably.

"So did mine, boy. Even so . . ." Uncle paused and clasped his hands behind his back. He made a point of staring directly into Dad's eyes. What Uncle had to say next was so important that Uncle used Chinese, but he spoke slowly so I could understand him as well. *"Recently I've thought about this. Thought about it very hard. Today I came to tell you what I think. You must be careful of old dreams, whether they were good ones or bad ones. You must be careful even if you think you have given up those dreams, because old dreams are like hungry ghosts. They do not rest until they eat up everything. Even someone's life. I can see that happening with your son. That's why I came here today."*

Dad frowned and his eyebrows shoved together. "Unh, yeah," he said uneasily.

Uncle smiled sympathetically. "Now I'm tired. I want to sit down." Uncle began to shuffle back toward the store. I let him go past. I waited to let Dad go past as well, but he motioned me to go on ahead. He had a very thoughtful expression on his face.

When we were back in the store, Uncle headed for the roll of butcher paper again. He sat down on it heavily and sighed. "The world changes so, so much." He pushed out his lips for a moment. "I'm one old man and I'm full of old ideas. New ideas, they don't find room inside me. But I think about this too . . . lately. The world changes and we should change with it." He nodded his head firmly. I think those last words were meant for me because Uncle finally glanced in my direction right then. "And how are you, boy?"

"Pretty good, Uncle," I said.

Uncle cleared his throat. "Are you going to be lazy anymore, boy?"

"Craig works hard every day, Uncle," Dad said.

221

"I mean about his lessons," Uncle snapped without looking at Dad.

"Lessons? What lessons?" Dad asked.

Both Uncle and I ignored Dad.

"I don't know, Uncle," I said. It annoyed me that Uncle *Quail* would pretend that it was all my fault that I wasn't swimming with him in his cove. But I remembered what Mom had said, so I tried to be patient.

"I think you need the exercise." Uncle tilted back his head to study me and a smile slowly spread across his face. "And maybe your friend does too. You bring this friend that plays such fine jokes with rocks." He scratched his cheek. "What is her name?"

"Kenyon," I said. "But are you sure this time you want to invite her?"

"I want to meet this person, this Ken-yon, who is as stubborn as me. I don't believe you." Uncle put a hand on my shoulder and gave it a squeeze. He had a strong grip for such an old man—a grip strong enough to hold on to a rock even when all the sea was pounding against him. Then, using my shoulder for support, he rose to his feet. "I see you and your friend Saturday afternoon."

"Will we go diving for abalone then?" I asked.

Uncle laughed and patted me on the shoulder. "You be more patient, boy."

Dad got up and dug his truck keys from his pocket. "Here, Uncle. Let me give you a lift back."

But Uncle gently shoved Dad away from the door. "I can find my own way, boy. I just follow my nose to the sea." Uncle threw his shoulders back. "I want you to talk to your boy." He waved his hand at us and shuffled out of the store slowly.

I didn't think Uncle would ever let me go diving for abalone with him. It was too good an excuse to make me visit him in the cove. But somehow it didn't seem very important—it wasn't like Uncle was trying to lie to me. After I'd thought about it for a while, I guessed Uncle probably believed what he was saying. But what would I have really used the abalone for—except maybe to show off? I didn't feel as if I had to do that anymore.

Dad struck a match and finally lit his cigar. He sucked at it once and then took it from his mouth as he exhaled slowly. Dad studied the fiery red tip of the cigar for a while. "I never thought I'd see the day when you could get that old man outside of his cove."

"He must have thought it was very important to tell Craig to invite Kenyon." Mom rubbed at a spot on the glass top of the counter.

"Yeah, I guess he did." Dad seemed impressed as he placed the cigar back between his lips and picked up the stool, carrying it around behind the counter again, where he set it down. Then he laid his cigar down in the ashtray. "So you like swimming, do you?" From a pile behind the counter, he picked up an empty cardboard carton that had once held twenty-four cans of Spam. If we flattened the empty cardboard boxes and tied them up, the garbage men would take them away. "Do you like swimming a lot better than basketball?"

I slipped around behind the counter to join Mom and Dad. I picked up an empty box that had once held forty-eight cans of tuna. "Yeah," I said, "a lot better than basketball." I turned the box upside down and forced my fingers between the bottom flaps. "Dad, I'm your son, but that doesn't mean I have to be like you in everything. I mean, basketball worked okay for you, Dad, but it doesn't work for me."

"I don't know. What did basketball ever do for me really?" Dad jerked his arm in toward his stomach, ripping one of the bottom flaps away from the others. "I mean, all those trophies and all I got to do was pick fruit or flowers, or be a houseboy. And then a maintenance engineer." Dad gripped one side of the box while he pulled at the other flap. It came away with a loud ripping sound. "And now this." Dad tried his best to smile cheerfully. "Though who knows where this will lead, right?"

"Right, Dad," I agreed quickly. My left hand held one of the bottom box flaps steady while my right hand pulled the other flap up.

Dad flattened the Spam box between his hands into a long, flat rectangle of cardboard and set it down temporarily on the countertop. "And who knows? Maybe you could be a champion swimmer, right?" I guess in his own way he was trying to make the best of the situation. He nodded his head and again asked, "Right, boy?"

I took my time collapsing the tuna box between my hands and sliding it over Dad's flattened Spam box. "Dad," I said slowly, "I like swimming for fun, not because I beat someone in a race."

Dad picked up an empty carton that had once held sardine cans. "You're not scared of people, are you, boy? I mean, you're gonna have to compete." He turned the carton upside down.

I reached around Dad and got an empty corned beef hash carton. "No, I'm not scared, Dad." I flipped the carton upside down and tried to tear the carton apart, but they must have put extra glue on to hold the flaps together. I gave a little grunt and pulled harder at the flaps, finally feeling one of them pull free. "It's like if someone wanted to race, I would. But even if I didn't come in first, I wouldn't feel like I was losing." I pulled the other flap free. "The main thing is to have fun."

Dad still gripped the bottom flaps of the sardine carton as if he'd forgotten all about what he was supposed to be doing. He seemed to look at me—really look at me for what I was, not for what he imagined me to be. "So it doesn't matter to you if you win or lose?" He gave a thoughtful shake of his head.

"Not really." I flattened the carton in my hands and added it to the pile.

Dad seemed to notice the box in his hands. Hurriedly he tore the flaps apart and flattened the carton. "Or," he went on carefully, "whether a person succeeded or failed? I mean, if a person didn't have a big house and a car and stuff like that?"

"How do you measure success anyway?" I took the flattened box from Dad's hands and put it on top of the pile.

"It only matters how much you're loved and respected." Mom reached out her hand toward Dad. Delicately her fingernails scratched the back of one of Dad's hands. "I think you're doing pretty good."

"Sure," I chimed in.

Dad trapped Mom's hand against his stomach with his other hand. "I guess I am." He winked at me. I think we both knew he and I were very different people. Too different to really understand each other well. But if we loved each other, we could accept the differences and the fact that we would never be much alike. I mean, I couldn't live my life the way he had and I think Dad finally knew he couldn't have lived his life the same way as me; but we could still like each other.

Dad let go of Mom's hand. "You know what? All these months we've been down here and we haven't gone to the beach."

Mom got out the ball of string from underneath the counter. "There was always work in the store, or we were feeling too tired."

Dad took the string from Mom. "Well, let's take the day off sometime. We'll go to the beach whether the sun's shining or not." With his left hand Dad lifted the pile of flattened cartons while his right hand wound the string around them. "Only I'm not too good at swimming," he warned me.

"Neither am I," Mom said. She got out a pair of scissors.

"We wouldn't have to go out too far." I put my finger down on the knot so Dad could finish tying it. "We could just go wading."

Dad held the knot taut while Mom cut the string. "In that case," he said, "let's close the store for the afternoon this Sunday. Then we could all go to the beach. We haven't done something as a family in a long time."

"It sounds good to me." I bent over and put a hand on either side of the stack and picked it up to carry out back.

IV

The next day at noon recess when I found Kenyon, I told her about Uncle's invitation.

She was sitting on a patch of lawn in the shade of the gym. She swung her head up suspiciously to look at me. "What made your uncle change his mind again?" She clasped the little turquoise medallion on her necklace and tugged at it gently, swinging her fist from left to right and back again.

I hadn't dared to sit down with her but was still standing. I shifted my weight nervously. "He doesn't have any real family and most of his friends are dead, so I guess he just got lonely."

Kenyon dropped her hand from her necklace and smiled. "Well, Fab-uu."

"What?" I asked. Apparently Kenyon had some new catchword.

Kenyon made a face. "Fab-uu is short for fabulous."

"Let's see." While I thought for a moment, my fingers

squeezed another fold on the mouth of my lunch bag. "I'll make Uncle's deliveries last. So I'll be by your house at about three in the afternoon. Okay?"

"Sure, fine." Kenyon spread open the mouth of her lunch bag. "Aren't you going to take a load off your feet and sit down?"

"Unh . . . well, I thought I'd see if Stanley and Sheila would like to go too. I mean, I don't think Uncle'd mind. We're kind of related." Actually, I figured Uncle wouldn't mind Stanley and Sheila because they were Chinese. "What do you think?"

"I don't know." Kenyon frowned at the carrot stick she'd taken out of her lunch bag. "Why don't you ask them?" She flung the carrot stick back into her bag.

"Watch my lunch, will you?" I set my lunch bag down beside her.

She grinned wickedly and wriggled her eyebrows up and down. "Sure, but there may not be much left."

"As long as there's something." I headed over to the playing field, where Stanley was throwing the baseball around with some of the other guys. They were warming up before they began choosing sides.

I stopped by the edge of the field and cupped my hands around my mouth. "Hey, Stanley."

Stanley caught the baseball with a loud cracking

sound. "You going to play?" he asked in an exasperated voice.

I tried not to sound hurt. "No. I just wanted to know if you wanted to visit Uncle *Quail.*"

"Hell, no." Stanley made a face as if I'd asked him to do something unpleasant like help take out the garbage.

"But—"

Stanley was already running toward the field. He turned around for a moment so that he was running backward. "I said no. N-O. No."

I shrugged and went back toward the school buildings, where Sheila was already playing volleyball. For a moment, I thought about just phoning her, because she was playing with the rest of her pack. But I remembered what Dad had said: that I shouldn't be afraid to show the kids who and what I was. Only I should have remembered what Mom had said about using a soft touch sometimes.

"Hey, Sheila," I called from the sidelines. "You want to visit Uncle *Quail*? It'd be fun."

Sheila waited, slightly hunched forward, ready for the ball to come to her. "You call that pain-in-the-ass fun? He's so weird, and he's always got some lecture to give me."

"But he might be able to help us with our project," I said. Mr. Loeb, our teacher, had this idea for a class project: We'd each of us write a one-page report about the ethnic group we came from; and then we'd get together by ethnic groups and do a short presentation in class.

Sheila jumped up high in the air and swung her fist against the volleyball with a loud thump as she spiked the ball into the opposing team's court. "I'm going to write about Grant Avenue, so I already know everything I need to know." She trotted into the back of the court as her team rotated.

"But that's just souvenir stores and restaurants." I stuffed my hands into my pockets. "That's not real Chinese."

Sheila crouched as the volleyball was served. "You just don't fit in. You make this big thing of acting like some Chinese clown, when we're Americans. Americans, do you understand?"

I frowned, puzzled, and with my hands still in my pockets, I moved my arms out away from my sides and then back in again—like a bird flapping its wings. "Why do you have to be one or the other? Why can't you be both?"

Sheila turned her head. "Boy, are you ever stu—" she began to say when the volleyball bounced in front of her.

"Oh, Sheila," Betsy said in disappointment.

Disgustedly Sheila caught the volleyball as it bounced

and she whirled around again. Clasping the volleyball tightly between her hands, she raised the volleyball over her head threateningly. "Just leave me alone, will you?"

But I stayed where I was. She had me and Uncle all wrong. "You're missing so much," I protested. "Like Uncle's—"

With all her strength, Sheila whipped the volleyball at me. "Get out of here."

I managed to duck just in time. I straightened while Betsy ran past me to get the volleyball. I stared at Sheila, shocked by how angry I had made her. Betsy had stepped back on the court with the volleyball by the time I'd worked up enough nerve to try to explain myself to Sheila. "But—"

Sheila ran toward Betsy and grabbed the volleyball from Betsy's startled hands. She threw the ball at me again with all her strength. "Get away from me," she said angrily.

This time I wasn't fast enough and it caught me on the heel. I bent over to rub my foot. "I . . . unh . . . yeah, if that's what you want." I found myself wandering back to where Kenyon was sitting. "Did you hear us?" I asked her. I was pretty shaken up by Sheila.

"Some." Kenyon was nibbling at half of a baloney-and-cheese sandwich that looked suspiciously like the one

Mom had made for me. "Couldn't help hearing the end of it though. I think most everyone in the school did."

"I just always seem to say the wrong thing to her." I sat down and checked my lunch bag. There was only half of a sandwich in there, and the chocolate chip cookies were gone.

Kenyon held her bag up to me. "You can have my alfalfa sprouts sandwich. And ALL my carrot sticks."

"No thanks." I noticed my chocolate chip cookies lying on a napkin beside Kenyon, and I liberated one of the cookies and leaned my head back to rest against the wall of the gym. "I don't know. When I'm around, my cousins get this kind of look. . . ." I took a bite from the cookie. "They look just like a cat when you rub its fur the wrong way."

Kenyon took a cookie from the napkin. "Well, maybe you really do make them nervous. I mean, you seem to like being Chinese."

I took the remaining half of my sandwich from the bag. "It's what I am."

Kenyon nibbled at the edges of her cookie. "And it's what Stanley and Sheila are, only they may not know it. Or they pretend they don't."

I took a big bite from my sandwich because I didn't like the hungry way Kenyon was eyeing it. "Why would

Stanley and Sheila pretend they aren't Chinese?"

Kenyon started to brush some of the crumbs from her lap. "Because maybe they think the other kids would make fun of them." She paused with her hand above her legs. "Not everyone likes to be different. It's easier to be the same as other people. Safer too. Only you remind them that they're not as white as they'd like to be." She picked up her lunch bag. "Sure you don't want some of mine?"

"Some other time." I shook my head.

"Yeah, sure." Kenyon flung her lunch bag toward the garbage can about five feet from us. It hit the sides heavily and carrot sticks and a plastic-wrapped sandwich fell on the ground. Kenyon scrambled to her feet and began to pick up her lunch.

It was right at that time that Bradley stalked over toward us. His hands clenched and unclenched nervously. I thought he had left the field because he was going to the water fountain, but he headed over toward us instead. Or rather he looked over toward us. "Aren't you going to play baseball? They're just starting to choose sides."

"No, I don't think so." I finished my sandwich and wiped my fingers on my lunch bag. "But thanks for asking. I don't like baseball much."

I expected Bradley to make some joke about my lousy

playing, but instead he just nodded his head in agreement. "Yeah. I don't like baseball much either. Everybody thinks that just because I'm big, I've got to hit a home run every time." For a big guy he had a funny little hoarse voice. "And if I strike out, sometimes even weeks later they don't let me forget I've been a goat."

I picked up a cookie from the napkin and stared up at Bradley in surprise. "I thought you liked all sports."

Bradley rubbed his cheek like a mosquito had just bitten him. "Sports just make me feel . . . well . . . bigger. I don't even like football much. Who wants to shove people around?"

I waved a hand at the shade. "Well, why don't you sit down instead of playing."

Bradley looked at the field, where they were still choosing sides; and then with a slow grin, Bradley lowered himself to the ground. "You know," he said in amazement, "it's just too hot a day to be running around in the sun."

Kenyon had finished picking up everything and throwing it away by that time. She sat back down and handed Bradley one of the cookies. "Here. You'll need some energy if you're going to sit here. We rest hard."

"Thanks." Bradley lifted the cookie in a salute to us and popped it into his mouth. Between chews, he said,

"Yes, sir. It's way too hot to be playing today." He kicked his legs out in front of himself.

The guys on the field had stopped choosing sides and were waving toward Bradley and shouting something, but their voices were lost in the wind. Bradley raised one hand and waved it from left to right to show he didn't want any part of the game today. Stanley trotted over toward us. I realized then that Stanley would probably never take a stroll someplace—he'd always be in too much of a hurry.

Stanley stood over us with his fists on his hips. He nodded impatiently to Bradley. "Hey, come on. The other side's got Powell. If we don't have you to even things up, we'll lose for sure."

Bradley slipped his hands behind his head and leaned back against the wall. "That's too bad, but you're going to have to find someone else."

Stanley shifted weight from one foot to the other. His voice took on a whining note. "You mean you'd just sit here and watch us lose?"

Bradley looked as if he were weakening—as if Stanley could shame him into playing—so I spoke up. "Why not? It's nice here in the shade."

"Keep out of this," Stanley snapped at me.

"Hey." Bradley sounded a little annoyed. "The three of us were talking before you barged in. Why don't you go back and play your game?"

But Stanley still would not give up. He spread his hands out from his sides. "Bradley, we can win if you play."

Kenyon sat up straight. "It isn't whether you win or lose, Stan," she said with mock sweetness, "it's how you—"

"Bullshit." In frustration Stanley whirled around on his heel and ran back to the game. There was some talk among the other guys and they all glared at us and Bradley.

Kenyon muttered from the side of her mouth. "Smile for the folks, Brad, and wave hello."

Brad tilted his head to his left and waved at them.

It's funny, but last December—well, even just a month ago—I would have given anything to be like Stanley and have all of his friends. But I realized right then that Stanley would never know what it meant to relax and enjoy a sunny afternoon. He would always be too busy looking for someone to beat in some game. You couldn't have paid me now to be like Stanley.

CHAPTER | X

"He's a little funny," I warned Kenyon in a whisper.

Kenyon was having no trouble following me down the path, though she was barefoot and the rocks were hot. "Yeah, how?" Kenyon sounded as if she were ready to match stories with me about eccentric relatives.

But I wasn't in the mood for more of Kenyon's stories. "Just don't be surprised by anything Uncle does." I figured it would be easier to let her see for herself.

After I had put the carton of groceries on the porch, I knocked at the door and Uncle took his time opening it. There was silence for a while. I motioned to Kenyon. "Uncle, this is my friend, Kenyon. Kenyon, this is Uncle *Quail*."

"How do you do?" Kenyon reached out her hand.

Uncle looked at her hand and then at her. "Are you a boy or a girl?" He frowned at her T-shirt and jeans.

"A girl, of course." Kenyon tried to make herself sound pleasant. She looked, though, as if she were having second thoughts about swimming in the cove.

Uncle looked over her shoulder at me and shook his head. "Things are very, very different now."

"Well, things aren't all that bad."

"Maybe," he grudged. "But they are not all good either." Uncle nodded at his house. "You can change in here," he told Kenyon. "We'll wait outside."

"I'm wearing my suit underneath my stuff already," Kenyon informed him.

"Mmph." Uncle shook his head and walked down the steps. "This way then."

Kenyon looked a little mad and she started to open her mouth but I touched her wrist. "Remember. I warned you," I whispered.

"You didn't tell me he was going to be an old fossil." Kenyon almost hissed the last word.

"He's old enough now to say what he wants."

Uncle was already down at the foot of the path. He turned. "You mean I survive. Let's see you survive as long as me, then you say what you want to."

Kenyon pulled her swimming cap out of her back

pocket. "Your uncle's got sharp ears," she said as she went down the path ahead of me. It seemed that Uncle had gone up a bit in her estimation.

Uncle was already in his trunks, so he folded his arms and stared seaward while we got ready. Without turning around, he asked. "You swim good, girl?"

"I swim laps in an Olympic-sized pool." Kenyon tucked the last bit of her hair underneath her blue cap.

"Sunshine swimming," Uncle said, "in tame water."

Kenyon didn't even bother answering Uncle. Instead she went past him, holding her arms out from her sides as she began high-stepping into the water. Uncle turned his head slightly to watch as Kenyon leaned forward and slid under the water. She turned onto her back when she surfaced, moving as easily as Uncle would have. Her arms rose leisurely like a swan's wings over her head as she drifted on her back.

"She can swim, that girl," Uncle said with quiet approval. He motioned to me. "Go on, boy." I went into the water. It was a little warmer than usual. I floundered and churned around when hands grabbed one of my ankles and I was pulled under.

I squinted under the water and saw a grinning Kenyon already rising for air. Her face was tilted up with a tiny stream of bubbles slipping from her nose, and her arms hung by her sides as she kicked her legs toward the top. I gave a kick toward where the lower half of her body seemed to be hanging from the surface. With her head above the water, she couldn't see me; but I knew I couldn't reach her because I had to surface for air myself.

When my head broke above the sea, I trod water for a moment, blinking my eyes. She wasn't anywhere to be seen, and then I felt something tug at my ankles again, flipping me backward under the surface. By the time I righted myself, Kenyon was already swimming away from me.

I surfaced before she could and swam a little way closer to her before her blue-capped head appeared above the water. Then I turned so I was floating on my back. When she finally surfaced, I began kicking my legs stiff and hard, raising sheets of spray that showered her. I caught her by surprise, I think, so she got some water right into her mouth when she was going to breathe. She began coughing and wiping at her eyes with one hand while she trod water. And then she turned her head to the side, holding up her hand and spluttering. "Enough."

I stopped. "Are you all right?"

She wiped at her eyes. "Yeah, no thanks to you." She

coughed again and spit some salt water from her mouth. She seemed to have lost her taste for pranks. She gave a kick that carried her over to the old pilings and held on to them.

"Are you feeling okay?" I swam over to her slowly.

She thrust out her chin. "All right enough to race you to the reef and back."

"Wait." Uncle swam over to where we were.

"Where shall we start?" I asked.

"From here." Kenyon gave a kick and ducked her head under the water for a moment as she raced toward the reef, but Uncle wasn't too far behind her. By the time I got started, I was following in the choppy water of their wakes.

Kenyon was the first one to touch the reef. I heard her wet palm slap against one of the rocks, but she made the mistake of turning to see how far ahead she was. Uncle touched the reef only a second later. He didn't do any fancy competition flips like Kenyon did but he still managed to turn around quickly enough. They wound up both kicking off from the reef at the same time. I had touched the reef and was halfway back by the time Kenyon reached the pilings ahead of Uncle, but it was a close thing and Kenyon had to swim hard.

"That was a good race," she panted to Uncle.

Uncle, treading water like she was doing, nodded his head. "You are one good swimmer." He drifted back a little and let me swim by to touch one of the pilings. I held on to it while I rested.

"Now tell me the truth," Uncle said to Kenyon. "You made that funny rock."

"Uncle thinks the fossil clam is just a carved rock," I explained to Kenyon.

"I found it," Kenyon said. "I got better things to do with my time than to go around fooling Craig."

"Maybe," Uncle said skeptically, but he didn't really seem to care one way or another.

For a little while after that, the three of us floated on our backs, feeling like otters or pieces of driftwood. Overhead, the sky was a bright, burning blue—like the blue heart you can see sometimes inside the yellow flame of some mechanic's torch just before he cuts through steel. The clouds were white and looked as if someone had combed them into long, slender, white strands that ran in parallel rows. Or like something else.

I said to Kenyon, "Don't those clouds look like furrows in a field?"

Kenyon kept herself more or less in the same position with lazy waves of her hands. "I don't know. They look more like the white threads on a pair of Levi's. You know, just around the knees. When all the vertical blue threads wear away."

"A piece of worn-out sky." Uncle laughed and paused. Almost regretfully, he added, "Well, it's time we went back." We turned and swam back toward the shining white sand. As we waded out of the surf, Uncle glanced at Kenyon and then at me. *"Maybe,"* he said in Chinese, *"maybe my father was wrong. The true victory is not to remember just the bad things. Someone must also remember the good things about this way of life."*

Kenyon spread her towel on the beach and lay down. "What did you say?"

I spoke before Uncle could. "Uncle was saying what a good thing it is to share an afternoon like this." With my towel around my shoulders, I sat down.

"Yeah, it is pretty good." Kenyon pulled off her cap and shook out her hair.

The three of us lay on our backs, letting the sun warm us for a long time. Finally, I rolled on my side, resting my head on one of my arms. The surf foamed and hissed up the sandy beach and I was just closing my eyes to sleep when I saw something gleam in the water. I got up. Whatever it was twinkled as it tumbled on the edge of the receding sea.

"What is it?" Kenyon asked.

"Something . . ." I said. I started down the wet sand across the froth that lay bubbling and popping on the sand. When I had waded into the ankle-deep water, I turned every which way trying to catch a glimpse of it again.

The tide surged in once more and still I couldn't see it. I twisted this way and that, trying to catch sight of it again, but I couldn't. The surf foamed about my knees for a moment and then as the sea seemed to sag away from the beach, I could feel the water tugging and sucking at my legs. I dug my heels into the wet sand as I looked around. The tide seemed to rush away even faster now.

Finally, I saw something shining farther over to my right. I splashed through the water as I ran. The light winked over and over as it rolled down the beach, following the edge of the sea. I bent over, my hands groping like crabs through the water as I followed the ebbing tide. The sea was flowing away even faster than before, leaving little bits of broken shell and small pebbles momentarily on the sand. The tide was so low on the beach now that there were little ripples on its surface like hen scratches.

I saw something gleam just ahead of me, and then it was gone again. I dug into the wet sand with my fingers, tugging something free just as the surf rushed back in.

The sea almost swept the thing from my fingers but I managed to hold on to it. Then when the force of the sea had lessened, I swirled the thing around in the water to wash away any loose sand before I waded back to the beach.

I walked along slowly as I stared at what I had in the palm of one hand. It was a flat, disklike object about the length of my thumb, and it seemed to be made of translucent, milky-green quartz.

By now Uncle and Kenyon were both sitting up. "What is it?" Kenyon called.

"I don't know. But it's no dragon's egg." I held it out for them to take a look.

"What do you mean by a dragon's egg?" Kenyon demanded.

"Ask Uncle about it sometime." I thought that now that Uncle had accepted Kenyon a little, he would be willing to pass on some of his stories. "But what do you think this thing is?"

Kenyon took it while I sat back down and threw sand on my legs to cover them with a warm coating.

"It's sea glass," Uncle declared.

"What?"

"Sea glass," Kenyon echoed Uncle. "Some people call it drift glass. Haven't you seen it before? Someone must have broken a Coke bottle a long time ago on a rock at a beach, and then some of the pieces must have gotten picked up by the sea. The tide washed the glass and polished the edges so that they're smooth and round now and not sharp. And it got washed into here finally."

"It looks more like a stone than glass." I put out my hand; and, when Kenyon had passed the sea glass back to me, I held it up toward the sun. The light shone through it softly onto the beach, so that it seemed as if there were a small jellyfish made of bright pale-green light on the sand.

"It's just junk," Kenyon said. "I've never found two pieces that were the same. The sea waves rub it and so does the sand on the beach."

I thought to myself, Until all that's left is the brightness and the clearness. To Kenyon I said, "It's pretty, though."

I put it by my towel to save.

AFTERWORD

Because sports don't always fit into the "exotic" image of Chinatown and the Chinese, I should state here that I did not invent the story of a professional Chinese-American basketball team. Though it did not receive much publicity, such a team did go on tour in the late 1930's, with members recruited from the amateur basketball teams in the various Chinatowns.